THE PECULIAR VANISHING ACT OF MR RALPH HERRIOT

A VICTORIAN MYSTERY

THE MRS IMOGENE LYNCH SERIES
BOOK 2

HANNAH IVORY

Some folk want their luck buttered.

— THOMAS HARDY

ISBN eBook: 978-90-833027-0-6
ISBN Paperback: 978-90-833027-2-0
Cover designer: EbookLaunch
Editor: Amber Fritz-Hewer
Website: Hannah Ivory

CATHERINE'S MOST PREPOSTEROUS PROPOSAL

Honeydew Mansion, Cotswolds, 20 April 1896

I have everything in the world a person needs: good health, a lovely home, a doting dog, a family who cares for me, and more than enough worldly goods to satisfy even a hungry soul. Yet, I'm as melancholy as an Irish melody.

I returned home to Honeydew Mansion after a prolonged stay in Dartmond in early February and the first weeks were happy, like the blessed above. I ached none for my cramped apartment over the Hopewell's Bookshop on Darren Street, watching the Dartmonders go from baker to butcher to grocer. Home was heaven and all I'd craved for.

Roly-Poly Jasper, my darling doggie, settled back in at home like he'd never been away. He is old though, as he now merely lifts his grey head to sniff the air when he gets the scent of a hare in his nostrils. Lying on the mat, he pricks up his ears, blinks, then back to sleep.

Don't get me wrong, I still think fondly of my maid Gertie and her beau Neil Fritter. And young Timothy Pocock, of course, has captured a place in my heart for good. Even my landlords, the Hopewells, despite our early squabbles, became quite good friends. My thoughts also frequently return to the languid Miss Platt and colourful mayor Rahul Banerjee.

But all of them are not as much missed as I had missed my home. Or at least what I thought was home. With Mrs Peaton singing in the kitchen and Jasper running around Tiversack Lake as a young puppy, life seemed to laugh at me again. With the drawn-out case of the secret Christmas baby finally solved, my conscience was clear. Having fulfilled my Thaddeus's last request, I knew it was the right thing to leave my Dartmond friends behind and return to my spacious, sun-filled villa with my own furniture and lovely garden.

Another recent delight was Cousin Catherine's stay with me at Honeydew Mansion for two weeks. It was sheer joy. We'd both forgotten how we used to dote on each other as children and though we'd missed most of each other's adult years, it was as if time had stood still for us. I was so sad when she left, but understood she had other obligations.

"Dearest Imogene, my brother will think we've fallen out with each other when I'm not at least spending some time at home with him and Anna at Gladmers Mansion. But do come and stay with me in London in the spring. Or even accompany me to Egypt when I return there in May." She'd laughed that captivating, tinkling laugh of hers, a sound that cannot help but make you smile as well, full of mirth and mischief.

She rubs the flour from her hands and then comes over to the sink to wash them.

"We're going to have a cuppa," is her curt reply.

"How have you managed here on your own, Mrs Peaton?" I ask in my turn, a question that was long overdue, but this is the first time we're actually alone in the house since my return from Dartmond.

Busy putting the kettle on and getting the teacups out, she doesn't immediately answer me, then looks straight at me with those clear blue eyes.

"It has been good and not so good, to tell the truth. The good thing is that I love this house and as it's so big, it's kept me busy. But it's been darn silent. I'm glad you're back, Mrs Lynch."

"Even when I'm not fantastic company?" I pull a face.

"Oh, but when Lady Lowther was here, you were perfect company, and it was so wonderful to cook for people besides myself again." My housekeeper looks at me with these knowing eyes. You cannot be in someone's service for over twenty-five years and not know them intimately. I know she doted on Thaddeus as well.

"Why don't you visit London this spring, Mrs Lynch?"

I shake my head.

"I can't, Mrs Peaton, and you know why. It's not proper to hop from one place to the other like a restless robin. I must get accustomed to being here on my own. And there are so many of Mr Lynch's things that I must clear out, like his desk and his wardro..." She raises a pudgy hand.

"Stop right there, Ma'am. Nobody says you must do these things right now. I'm dusting the constable's office every week and I air his clothes regularly, so there will be no moths in them."

"But..."

"But you'd rather be miserable?" She interrupts me, "Grieving one's husband takes years. And I was only married to Mr Peaton for five years when he was killed in the Crimean War. Yet, I was so grateful that you took me in, and I didn't have to stay in our silent marital home any longer. I think it is the same for you, Mrs Lynch. You'll feel better when you're away. In time, it will be easier and easier to come here."

"But what about you? I can't leave you running the house on your own once again?"

Mrs Peaton pours us the deliciously smelling Darjeeling tea in my favourite Wedgewood cups. I surely missed those in my rented apartment over Hopewell's Bookshop.

"That's what I've been wanting to discuss with you, Mrs Lynch."

My eyes grow wide with trepidation. If she's going to leave me now, I'm going to collapse on the spot. Jasper seems to sense my distress and firmly places his snout on my shoe.

"Are you...?"

"No, no, don't worry. I've met someone." Mrs Peaton's round face turns crimson and my heart skips a beat. *She couldn't have found love again!* But then the next wave of fear washes over me. In that case, she will certainly leave me.

"Who is it?" I inquire with interest. "Someone I know?"

Mrs Peaton dips her head as if ashamed. Why would

anyone be ashamed of love, the most precious of human feelings?

"It is, Mrs Lynch, it is..." she hesitates, looks out of the freshly washed windows with the white lace curtains. "It is Bernie Craig, your gardener."

"Bernie?" I take a minute to visualize the stout, ruddy, short-legged Bernie, who's as silent as the elves, as Mrs Peaton's beau, but then the penny drops.

"Of course!" I cry out, "I had totally forgotten he's a widower with two grown sons. Oh, I'm so happy for you!"

Mrs Peaton looks as if a thirty-pound sack of flour has taken off her shoulders.

"Really?" Her sweet face with the light eyes gleam with pleasure. "I wasn't sure how you would take it. I wanted your approval first, and nothing's going to change. We're not starting a family at our age," she points to her greying hair. "And we would just like to keep looking after Honeydew Mansion for you as we've done for years."

While I'm feeling relieved of my own burden, my mind races.

"You'll both stay at the cottage, of course. It hasn't been used for ages, but I'm sure Bernie can do it up nicely for you both."

"Oh, we'd hoped you'd say that, Mrs Lynch, but it's really no trouble for me to keep living in the house and if you'd be in London for a while it might actually be safer to have someone in the big house."

"When are you planning on getting married?"

"Now we have your consent to our courtship, Ma'am, we can start planning the event. But really, we are in no rush. Though Bernie and I enjoy each other's company, he's quite content in his house in town and I'm happy where I am."

"Just make sure you invite me to the wedding!"

"Of course. I'd love for you to be my witness, if you would, Mrs Lynch."

"That would be marvellous! Oh, you've certainly made my day, Mrs Peaton! Or should I call you Mrs Craig now?"

"Mrs Peaton for you always, Ma'am."

My melancholia temporarily melts away at this blissful announcement of new love found at a mature age.

At that moment, the door knocker comes down twice on the front door.

"Who can that be?" I wonder aloud. Mrs Peaton's deliveries are always brought to the back door, and we're not expecting visitors. I just felt perked up enough to take Jasper for his walk.

"I'll have a look." Mrs. Peaton puts her teacup down and takes off her apron.

2

THE CONSPIRACY OF FRIENDS

Honeydew Mansion, later the same day, 20 April 1896

Seconds later, I'm surprised to hear Doctor Rule's familiar voice asking if I'm home. My GP's arrival instantly alarms me something is wrong with Finley or Anna. Or God forbid, Catherine.

"Imogene!" The jovial Ed Rule comes towards me and grabs both my hands. No sign of a calamity there.

"Ed? What brings you here?" I smile in return, always pleased to see my white-haired doctor, who is also my friend and with whom I shared so much when Thaddeus fell ill.

"I was passing by after seeing a patient and I have a spare hour. I know you usually go for your morning walk with Jasper and the weather is so inviting, so I was wondering if I could accompany you on your walk?"

I raise one eyebrow. This is very un-Doctor Rule-like. Also not speaking in short, staccato sentences...hmmm? I feel I'm putting up my investigation cap, but I say nothing.

"Absolutely. I was just on my way out."

Jasper is wriggling his roly-poly body in delight at the word "walk". He likes the Doctor, but he enjoys rushing along the shoreline even more.

As soon as we're out of earshot from the house, I fire my question. "What is this about, Ed? Let the cat out of the bag."

"There's no sugar-coating with you, Imogene, is there?"

"No, there isn't." I say with a little laugh.

"I'm worried about you."

As if he's the investigator now, he doesn't say more, which forces me to ask.

"What about?"

"Your mental wellbeing. After the first rough and tumble of mourning, grief becomes more of a cyclic affair. As Thaddeus passed away last spring, this spring is going to be the hardest for you. You've come full circle, so to say. That's what you are experiencing now."

I'm listening intently to his words. I hadn't thought of grief as a cycle myself, but it makes sense. It is as if my body remembers that a year of day after day without my benedict has passed.

"So that's it?" I'm thinking aloud, my eyes watching Jasper splash through the cold water as if he's a pup all over again.

"Yes, that's it, Imogene."

"Well, I'll just have to grasp the nettle and live with it. What choice do I have?"

"Distraction. New surroundings."

I can't help but laugh out loud.

"You must have been talking with Cousin Catherine, Ed."

He shrugs his shoulder, halts in the sand, and looks at me squarely. The honey-brown eyes probing me.

"What if I have?"

I stop as well, taking in my surroundings. I feel the heaviness of my heart, the emptiness, the pain.

"But Cairo, Ed? For sure not Cairo?"

"Yes Cairo, Imogene. London has memories for you as well. You need to go where you have no memories. That's why Dartmond worked for you last year. But now, go for a vacation, enjoy yourself, free yourself, so to speak."

"But I can't, Ed. I can't leave Mrs Peaton to look after the house on her own again. And what about Jasper?"

The Doctor follows my eyes and watches Jasper snapping at the foamy waves.

"Jasper goes where you go, Imogene. Don't worry about him."

"But he's old." I feel like I'm running out of options.

"They have veterinarians in Egypt. And also aboard any ship that has foot passengers."

"How do you know that?" I become suspicious.

"I didn't. Catherine found out."

I sigh and call Jasper to my side who leaves the shoreline reluctantly.

"You two seem to have been conspiring together and have it all mapped out for me. I'm not sure I like it," but I say it with a grin.

Now it's the Doctor's time to sigh.

"I know it's a big step for you, Imogene. But you told me you used to travel with your parents before you were married, and you and Thaddeus did have an extended honeymoon in Italy."

Flashes of memories flood back to me - scents, sounds, and colours. Marrakech, New York, Biarritz, Nice. And, of course Florence, Rome, Venice... Hanging onto Thaddeus's arm in my white silk dress with matching hat. A young bride, giddy with love.

Could I? Should I?

"Let me sleep on it" My voice is husky and emotional.

"That's all I'm asking of you as my friend and my patient. And have a talk with Julietta. Being from Greece, my wife has travelled to Egypt often. She can tell you what it's like if you fear Catherine only paints too pretty a picture."

"I will do that." I say, "And thank you, Ed. Catherine would never have persuaded me, but you..."

That night lying in my bed feeling the empty space next to me, my mind roams my wardrobe - what to wear, what to purchase in London, on our way to the desert of Africa... But, no! It's preposterous! I can't possibly traipse around the globe at my age with an elderly dog in tow..."

But what if...?

I DECIDE NOTHING. I may or may not be going to Cairo. Maybe...

3

IS THERE STILL A WAY OUT?

Honeydew Mansion, two weeks later, 3 May 1896

It's a crisp and dewy morning in early May. Just the weather I enjoy here in the Cotswolds. As I step out onto the lawn that slopes down to Tiversack Forest, the morning sun dances like a gold-winged fairy over my garden. Once, this garden was Thaddeus's pride and joy, now it's mine. An abundance of life and colour in the walled kitchen garden and the flowerbeds around the perfectly manicured lawn.

The air is filled with the sweet fragrance of the magnolia and hyacinths, with here and there an early tuberose. Scent is such a comforting reminder of spring's beauty lifting the veil of grief that always seems to hit me harder in the mornings.

"Come, Jasper," I call to Roly-Poly as he lingers behind, sniffing the boxwood hedge intently where no doubt a hare has passed through in the night. Armed with my garden stool, basket, and snippers, I make my way towards the flower beds at the end of the extensive garden, next to Thaddeus's greenhouse, the soft gravel crunching under the soles of my garden shoes. Jasper now trots by my side, his plumy tail wagging in delight.

"Are you happy being back at Honeydew Mansion, my dear?" I can't help asking, sharing in the dog's simple delight in the garden. "It's alright. I'll say a firm 'no' to Catherine's ungodly plan to whisk us off to Egypt. I promise! The two of us belong here. Nowhere else. What was I thinking?"

Jasper is no longer listening, wandering off along the rose beds, sniffing here and there until his ears perk up as he spots a cabbage butterfly fluttering past. With a burst of energy, he chases after it, barking playfully as the white wings disappear over the hedge. I watch my darling dog fondly, a smile tugging at my heart. It's Jasper's friskiness that reminds me to embrace life's simple pleasures.

"I won't go to silly Egypt!"

My mind is made up as I lower myself to sit down on the garden stool. As my gloved hands run through the soil, I relish the soft coolness and promise the fresh earth holds. From the wicker basket, I pick up a tiny Damask rose, which promises to have rich pink flowers next year. As I cradle the plant in my hands as a new-born, I study it with interest. Again, there's that promise of a new life. My retrieved life at Honeydew Mansion.

"You will find a new home among the others, little rose," I say aloud, not worrying I must sound daft talking to a plant. There's still a hole where last year's rose died and Bernie, my gardener, pulled it out. Feeling the soil give way beneath my touch is like a minor act of creation amidst the void that loss and death leaves behind.

Returning my attention to the task at hand, I carefully place the Damask rose into its designated spot, then gently pat the soil around the base. It stands prim and small like an innocent schoolgirl, but I can already see its promise - the pink blossoms gracing the green branches, sweet perfume wafting up in the air - a testament to the resilience of nature. Despite my aching heart, this garden serves as a sanctuary, a place where life continues its eternal cycle despite the sorrows that befall us.

"Thank you, my benedict," I say wholeheartedly, and the wind waves the crown of the chestnut tree, answering my prayer.

Still sitting on my gardening stool, I almost feel like a proper rosarian, planting a new rose here and there. This was my Thaddeus's domain, the flowerbeds, but it's mine now. I look around me. It's still too early for most roses to bloom, but the bright yellow Canary Birds are already popping open, as are the early peonies. Tending to the bigger bushes, I will leave for Bernie.

"I'll prune those, Mrs Lynch," he'd told me while spitting a firm splurge of red chewing tobacco onto the lettuce bed he'd just prepared. "You take them dead leaves and branches out of the geraniums and leave them prickly bushes to me."

And that's just what I'll do now, while Jasper is rolling on his back on the lawn, getting thoroughly wet and muddy. But instead of scolding him, I let him be his roly-poly self. I'll sort him out when we get back to the house for lunch.

As I check the potted geraniums Bernie has brought onto the terrace from the greenhouse, I listen to the silence. It's been a tough decision, but I sold all of Thaddeus's canaries last week. Bernie tended to them as best as he could, even when I was in Dartmond solving the secret Christmas baby affair, but there comes a point one has to acknowledge the past is the past. The canaries were Thaddeus's thing, not mine, and the poor birdies weren't getting any happier without the Master. They were actually an altogether sad bunch.

"Mrs Lynch, I might just have found the right place for them," Bernie announced last week as he came for his daily round of feeding them. "Young Fitzpatrick, you know the postmaster's son, has shown an interest in them. His parents were against it at first, but when I assured them you didn't want any money for 'em, they agreed he could have them as long as he would take good care of them."

I had been taken by surprise. Suddenly the idea of not hearing their chirping and fluttering made me sick in the stomach, but Mrs Peaton, who'd been listening to the conversation, had immediately chimed in.

"I'd say yes, Mrs Lynch, it will be one less worry on your plate, especially now you're going to travel to them faraway places like Egypt."

"But there's no Egypt on the cards now," I mumble.

Anyway, the canary move had been settled. Last Saturday, Fitzpatrick, a tall young man all legs and arms with a mop of black curls, had come over with his parents' cart and horses and taken the fifty canaries, cage and all.

As I rise to my feet, brushing the dirt from my skirts, I take a moment to survey the garden's developing beauty, while accepting the absence of canary song. Now it's just the silence of flowers and bushes, early lilacs, late tulips.

Jasper returns from his playful romp, his tongue lolling out in contentment. With a gentle pat on his head, we make our way back toward the house, our gardening session ended for now. I know that tomorrow we will return to this haven of blossoms and blooms to find solace in the ever-changing tapestry of nature's embrace.

"I'm going to be the gardener the Master would've been proud of. Proud as if I was becoming a second Gertrude Jekyll. Though, of course, I'll never be anything near that famous horticulturist," I tell Jasper as I slip off my soiled gloves and put them in the basket with the shears. He just wags his tail, not understanding what my nonsense babbling is about. Just the way I like it.

"Immy!" Cousin Caroline dashes around the corner of the house and strides towards us. "Guess what I found! Tickets to Brindisi! For next to nothing!"

"And what may Brindisi be, my dear? The latest London show?"

My joke even makes my forthright cousin stop in her tracks and eye me for a moment in sheer disbelief. Then she bursts out laughing.

"You're a funny one, Imogene." She gives me a sideways look with her green eyes as she pecks me on the cheek.

"I hope you've started packing because the steamship for Alexandria leaves the port on 8 June. Can you imagine, we'll be in Egypt by July. It will be sweltering hot, of course, but who cares? It's no use visiting the pyramids in winter. Then life's is as dead as a doornail in Egypt. One simply *has* to be there in season. Tout London knows that."

"Well, I'm not Tout London, dear Cousin. I'm not even

Tout Landdulton, for that matter," I retort drily, but Catherine is on one of her unstoppable spurs. Grabbing me under the elbow, she steers me to the backdoor.

"I've got it all in my bag and I rushed over to show you. Are you not a tiny bit pleased to see me, Immy? I thought you were as enthusiastic about our trip as I am. I can't wait to show you what's the most endearing place in the world for me."

"I will be more pleased if you stop using that silly name for me. Nobody calls me Immy these days, Catherine. I'm not twelve anymore. And Egypt doesn't equal endearing in my mind. I was actually just admiring my budding rose garden."

Catherine stops in her tracks, her long legs suddenly still. "Are you saying what I think I'm hearing? You won't come? You have second thoughts? You're ducking out?" Her face, still pretty and smooth as polished marble falls and she almost looks like Japer does when he's not getting a morning biscuit.

"Oh, Catherine, let's have tea and talk it over. You always go too fast for me. I'll ask Mrs Peaton to put on the kettle."

"I'd rather a brandy than a cup of tea. I feel like I'm being slapped in the face." Catherine grumbles as I hold the door open for her and step out of my garden shoes. I leave my wicker basket at the backdoor and go over to the sink to wash my hands.

Catherine is striding into my sitting room as if she owns it. Before I'm even in the room, I hear her uncorking the brandy bottle. Seriously? I hope my cousin hasn't got a drinking problem. What lady drinks at eleven in the morning?

4

A DIFFICULT CROSSING

British Channel Crossing, the morning of 20 May 1896

What have I done? What was I thinking? Why did Catherine and I have to cross the English Channel on the one morning in May it's storming? I don't believe I've ever been sicker in my life and those waves just won't calm down. I'm like a buoy bobbing up and down, but a buoy hasn't got a stomach full of tea and crackers. Oh, I'm so sick and I can't even take care of dear Jasper as all I can do is stay in my cabin and be nauseous. And then, I'm saying it in a polite way.

Catherine has the stomach of a sailor, apparently, which has one advantage. She's taking care of Jasper. But that gives me new worries. My cousin is not a dog person - I don't think she's had an animal in her life - and she's prone to these sudden silly ideas. Feeding the old dog something unfit or holding him over the railing to sniff the sea air. Oh! Oh! Oh! Dear God, please calm these waves or I'm sure I'll die.

In the spare moments I can put two thoughts together, I wonder how I'm ever going to survive this journey. Why did Doctor Ed and my cousin talk me into this Egypt mania? Oh, there's a calmer patch. Let me try to raise myself and gaze through the porthole. France, for sure, can't be far off now. I can't recall having longed for steady soil under my feet. One takes those normal conditions for granted.

Yes, I see the rocky French coast but it's still daringly far off. The strange thing is, I don't remember being sick on my honeymoon when Thaddeus and I took this same ferry, the *Dover Belle*. But then again it was quieter summer weather. Also, the time I travelled with my parents to India I distinctly remember dear Papa saying I had "sea legs just like him." Perhaps this seasickness is old age, but I put it down to the storm.

"Oh Immy, look at you! Poor thing. You look like a rag doll." Catherine comes in, all boisterous and healthy, her blonde hair in disarray and a smile on her pretty face.

"Where's Jasper?" I ask anxiously.

"Don't worry, dear. He's with the Captain. Unlike you, Jasper loves a good sea voyage and when I made a trip around the deck with him, Captain Monroe - whom I may call an acquaintance by now as I've been on the *Dover Belle* so often – fell in love with Jasper and I presume the love was mutual."

"What are you babbling about?" Another wave makes me lie down but I believe my eyes have the required sternness because Catherine quickly adds, "Jasper's just enjoying the view sitting on top of the bridge and I've made Captain Monroe swear he wouldn't feed Jasper anything, as you wouldn't approve of it."

"Oh Catherine, what have you done? Leaving my poor old dog with a stranger? Please go and fetch him for me."

Catherine stares down on me with a puzzled look on her face. Her bewilderment is genuine.

"Imogene dear, you're always so suspicious when it comes to men. Nathaniel is absolutely adorable. He's even got the twinkling blue eyes with all those lines at the temples, the white beard and hair, as you would expect from a sea captain. Add a clay pipe and Captain Monroe could be on a cover of a boys' novel on sea travels."

"I couldn't care less if he was Captain James Cook himself, Catherine. I would get up myself to retrieve my Roly-Poly from his perilous situation, but I'm really incapacitated."

"Alright, alright. Don't work yourself up. You look green around the gills anyway. I'll cut Jasper's adventure short but don't start moaning when he's with his nose at the door for the rest of the journey because he wants a sea view."

When Catherine is gone, the door to our cabin blown shut by the next gust of wind and another keeling of the ship that makes me send prayers upwards, I struggle to find the key to who my travel companion really is.

How well do I know Catherine? True, she's good fun and we had wonderful times when we were young, but she's been away for decades, and she definitely shares some traits with her mother, Lady Lowther, such as being rather rash and rakish.

I mean, is she even still married to Conservative MP

Sir Stafford Northwind? As far as I know she calls herself by her maiden name, Lowther. We saw the husband maybe twice after they got married and he's made quite a name for himself in London politics. Sir Northwind's name is all over the papers, being the Chancellor of the Exchequer. I wonder if there will come a moment that I feel at liberty to ask Catherine about her marital state. It seems such a delicate matter.

Anyway, I guess I'll have a hard time keeping up with my energetic and slightly unbridled cousin. I pray to God we don't end up in some sort of rigmarole we can't get out of.

Minutes later not only is the French coast very near, but my Roly-Poly returns to me with all his limbs intact, looking quite content. Maybe Catherine is right after all, and I'm the one who's the difficult traveller. With the horizon in view and Jasper in my lap, I express my remorse.

"Thank you for taking care of Jasper, Catherine, and my apologies for having doubted you. This travelling is all rather new to me, and I was really feeling under the weather."

Catherine waves a long-fingered, slim hand. "No need to make a fuss. I know you, remember? You were always the cautious one and it may actually serve me well on this trip. I didn't tell you I have an important mission in Egypt that I can't mess up." She looks at me conspiratorially and I feel the hairs in my neck stand up. All my premonitions are back.

"What are you saying, Catherine? I thought you said we were going on a vacation? I don't like, at all, what you're implying, nor the way you're looking when you say these mysterious things!"

"Oh, Immy, you always expect the worst. We *are* going on a vacation. It's just that I have to …uh…bring some…uh…things back to England with us and…they're sort of costly so I'm glad you're with me because you're the level-headed one and will steer us through."

"What kind of "uh things" are you talking about, Catherine?" I realise my voice is dark and even Jasper raises his snout and looks at Catherine.

But at that moment the ferry docks in the Port of Calais and we have to follow the porter, who brings our luggage to the train that will take us to Paris. I swear I will get to the bottom of this before we've left Paris. I can easily travel back myself if I don't like the sound of Catherine's wheelings and dealings.

5

A GLIMPSE OF THE REAL CATHERINE

The Train from Calais to Paris, the evening of 20 May 1896

I decide not to let the uncertainty about my cousin's mysterious plans rest, as I need an answer before we arrive in Paris. Then I can make up my mind whether to pursue this Egyptian adventure with her or to return home immediately.

Feeling remarkably revived as soon as I feel solid terrain under my feet, and my stomach settling as baby birds in the nest, I suggest to Catherine we head straight to the dinner compartment for our evening meal. We'll have at least five hours before we arrive in Paris around midnight.

"Fine," Catherine agrees. "I'm glad you're feeling better." After a quick stroll with Jasper outside the station, we board the Calais-Paris Express. Our luggage is already safely stored in our compartment, with the hatboxes on top.

"I crave lamb chops," I assert, surprised at my own appetite which usually is next to zero.

"Just pray the cook slaughtered a lamb before getting on the train," Catherine jokes.

"Oh, Cousin!" I cry out disgusted. "Why did you have to say that? Now my whole appetite has vanished."

"Sorry. Couldn't help myself," she answers with a lopsided smile. "I'll have some lamb myself, don't worry."

We're some of the first passengers to be seated in the first-class dining carriage, which has quaint square tables attached to the floor with bolts but decked with pristine white damask. The tables are set with porcelain plates, silver cutlery and crystal glasses. They are even decorated with small flower arrangements, but no candles. The chairs are understandably heavy and difficult to move.

A lanky, middle-aged French waiter with a dissatisfied frown on his elongated face helps us, pushing in our chairs, constantly mumbling *"alors mesdames, alors mesdames"* as if we're already too much for him at the beginning of his shift. Jasper gets a seat to himself and curls up in a bundle, too tired to even pretend to listen to our conversation.

Seconds later, the sedate waiter returns with a decanter of water and a notepad to take our orders. Catherine and I have settled on just a main course, the *Blanquette de Veau*, a veal stew, as there was no lamb on the menu.

"It comes with rice, Mesdames, not potatoes," the waiter warns us in his weary voice, as if he's convinced British ladies will insist on potatoes with every meal and he'll be blamed for bringing the wrong dish.

"That's fine," I answer chirpily for both of us and

Catherine nods. "Not keen on potatoes anyway," she informs the waiter who now looks as if he's between a rock and a hard place.

"Wine?" he inquires.

"I'll have a sherry, medium dry, to start. We'll see to wine with the dinner." Catherine takes the lead now.

"And you, Madame?" The waiter taps his pen on the notepad with agitation, making clear he wants me to make up my mind fast.

"I'll have the same. A small sherry."

I'm not sure this is a good idea on an empty and previously upset stomach.

"That'll settle your insides before you eat," Catherine observes, as the waiter skurries off to what I assume is the bar and kitchen compartment.

When we're settled with our aperitif and I feel a little more audacious after the first sip, I'm ready to leave the crossroads and get my answers.

"How many times have you been to Egypt, Cousin?"

I hope this is the right approach to getting Catherine to expand on her mysterious claim of having to bring things from Egypt to England.

She studies me over her glass. The green gaze is shrouded. Then she shrugs.

"I might as well share my Egypt story with you, now you're going to be a part of it," she sighs.

"Please do," I encourage, taking another firm sip of the sweet sherry that immediately goes to my head, but not in an unpleasant way, while the turbulence in my stomach calms down.

Catherine stares out of the window for a spell, then turns her eyes to me again. "I never planned to travel as much as I did. I wanted kids, a family, the whole wifey thing. But it wasn't to be."

"I'm so sorry." I bit my lip, wondering why I've never known this and whether I should have. I always thought Cousin Catherine had no homemaking skills and her traipsing around the world was her passion.

"No need to feel sorry for me, Immy. I've had a wonderful life. So far."

"So, what happened? Couldn't you and Staf...?"

But she cuts me short. "Stafford and I have a marriage of convenience. Let's call it that. Stafford isn't a ladies' man if you understand what I mean."

I don't. I've never heard of a husband who isn't a ladies' man. It's probably got something to do with men and politics. Catherine's tone is terse, so I don't want to ask the wrong question.

"Then I met Cornelius. Never mind his last name. Married too. Like me, a complicated marriage, the details of which are just as sordid. But never mind that. We fell in love. C and I are soulmates. We call each other C&C."

Catherine pauses. There's something diffident in her normally brazen look. As if she's afraid I'll judge her. And though I'm usually quite judgmental, I'm now listening with open ears. My main concern is my own ignorance of my cousin's troubled marriage. If only I had known.

Meeting Thaddeus at her and Stafford's wedding and our marriage being such a happy affair - though cut short by my benedict's untimely passing - I simply had assumed the same for Catherine. But if I had given it a thought, I should have contemplated there might be issues, with an earlier reference to "estranged marriage" popping up when the Northwinds' nuptial bonds were discussed. Which was once upon a time, a long time ago. Catherine was Catherine, travelling to exotic places while Stafford Northwind MP had his life and work in London.

I wait, hoping our closeness in the swaying carriage and the sherry will make Catherine disclose more and alleviate my guilt for being such an unsupportive cousin over the years.

While we're interrupted several times by the lanky waiter shuffling around us and bringing or taking plates and glasses, I get as much of the picture as Catherine is willing to tell me.

"The first time C and I went on a trip together outside England was in New Zealand. He's a historian and an archaeologist. He was going to New Zealand to study the Māori culture, as he was to organize an exhibition for the British Museum. On a whim, I accepted his invitation to come along. We weren't romantically involved at the time, just very good friends. And Stafford didn't seem to care the slightest. In fact, he encouraged a trip that would take me away for almost a year." Catherine stops, takes a large sip of Bordeaux wine, and dabs her mouth with the serviette. She looks almost helpless.

I keep silent, wondering what it must be like to travel to the other side of the world and below the equator with someone who's not your husband. I already thought India with my parents was the trip of a lifetime, but New Zealand?! I study my adventurous cousin with even more interest.

"It was heaven," Catherine sighs. "I loved C so much and I loved living among the Māori's. They're wonderful people. I even got the basics of their language, and I helped C with his collection. It was my first introduction into folklore and ancient art. He always says I have a knack for finding the rare pieces. And that I was able to get a good price due to my people's skills!" Catherine smiled at the remembrance. "I just loved what I did, where I was and with whom I was. Finally, far, far away from home, I was happy." Sadness glides over her attractive face and I presume the love story didn't have a happy ending. But I keep quiet.

"For the first time in my life, I was able to forget my unorthodox upbringing with a mother in an asylum and a distant father. Though we try, I've never been really close to my adopted brother Finley. And I certainly managed to marry the wrong man in Stafford Northwind." Again, I feel that bitter pang of remorse sweeping through Catherine and I want to help her.

"*We* used to be close," I blurt out despite myself.

"We used to. Until you married Thaddeus."

And like an oyster, Catherine snaps shut.

6

THE DECISION

Hôtel de Crillon, Paris, the next day, 21 May 1896

"Oh, how I love Paris! I wish we could stay here for a week!"

The next day Catherine is her breezy self again, making no further referral to the curt way in which she ended our conversation in the Calais-Paris Express dining carriage.

I've lain awake most of the night pondering the years when we hardly saw each other. It's true she sent us the occasional letter and when postcards came in vogue in recent years, we got one from Egypt and one from Greece. But how could I have replied? There was never an address on them. It's true I considered them rarities and didn't pay much notice to Catherine' signs of life.

So, her remark that we were close until I married was true. I was focusing on Thaddeus at the expense of the Lowthers. But was I the only one to blame? It was never clear where she was. Still, I could have reached out to Stafford to find out. Maybe this trip is my way to make up my neglect to Catherine. Maybe I should stop my dilly-dallying whether to return home.

"I love Paris, too," I reply meekly as I stroke Jasper's soft ears and enjoy the real French café au lait.

"Is something the matter? Did last night's meal not agree with you?" The green gaze rests on me intently and at that moment I realize I'm the only one who slept badly. Catherine may have snapped at me, but she has already totally forgotten the incident. She was just done talking at that moment. Catherine Lowther is not spiteful. Neither is she worrisome like me. She's a distinctly different person altogether.

"I'm fine," I reply, quickly making up my mind to stop my worries and just enjoy the trip, whatever it may bring. But as ever, Catherine takes me by surprise.

"Is it Thaddeus you miss, dearest Immy?" Her voice is warm and genuine. And her question moves me. I hadn't even realized I'd lain awake thinking about my benedict as well.

"It is. The only time I was in Paris was with Thaddeus. When we were on our honeymoon, on our way to Italy."

Catherine nods. "Paris *is* romantic. One feels things here one normally wouldn't. Maybe it's a good thing then we're only passing through and our sleeper train for Marseille leaves this afternoon."

"When was the last time you were here, Catherine?" I divert the attention from my memories.

A broad smile lights up her face. "Better ask, when wasn't I here? I pass through Paris every time I go to

Cairo, and I've been to Egypt six times in the past decade. You could say I'm a regular. This same hotel, even!. Hôtel de Crillon at the Place de la Concorde."

I don't dare to ask if she stayed here on her own, but I needn't have wondered.

"C and I found this hotel when we first touched base in Paris on our way to Cairo. Already then, De Crillon was *the* place to stay for international travellers. I have fond memories here too."

"Shall we go for a walk in the Jardin de Tuileries?" I suggest. "The weather is so nice and Jasper needs to stretch his legs, as well."

"Perfect idea," Catherine is already all energetic bustling. "I've ordered for our luggage to be taken to Gare de Lyon and the carriage will pick us up back here at noon."

As we walk side by side under the thick foliage of the elm trees down the Grande Allée, Catherine puts her arm through mine. I enjoy her closeness and her vivacity. I firmly decide to put all my last worries about Egypt to rest. But one should never underestimate my cousin!

"I promised you I would tell you why I need to go to Egypt this time," she begins out of the blue.

"Oh yes, of course," I'm taken by surprise.

Apparently, my startled voice makes her giggle. "Immy, Immy, you're such an open book. And I suppose that's why I love you. You're so straightforward, never with a secret."

I ponder this observation and suppose Catherine is right. I've made it my life's duty to be transparent and kind and reliable. That's how I want people to see me. But is there not a seed of unpredictability in me as well? I mean I'm walking here in the Jardin de Tuileries, without my Thaddeus, on my way to Africa! Isn't that a tad capricious? I wait for Catherine to continue.

"I told you I used to travel to several continents with C. In 1884, Sir Charles Newton, you know, the British Museum Director, sent C to Egypt to oversee the excavations at the Pyramids near Giza. C wasn't exactly an Egyptologist, but with decades of experience as an oversees archaeologist responsible for collecting cultural, heritage artifacts from all over the world, Sir Newton thought him a sound choice. But the relationship between Britain and Egypt was complex and we didn't know we'd be in for a ride." Catherine stops talking, a frown between her fair brows.

"Are you alright?" I ask.

"Yes."

"Jasper is tired. Let's sit down here." I sit down on a wooden bench in the shade. My Roly-Poly is unaccustomed to all the new smells and sounds, and it has exhausted him. He collapses at my feet instantly. Catherine sits down next to me.

"I'll try and keep it short. For some reason telling you the background takes ages."

"Oh, but I find it all very fascinating," I reply. "And as you seem to be going there on some sort of business, I might as well know what to expect." I don't dare to ask if the much-mentioned Mr C will be in Cairo as well. Either Catherine tells me, or it will be another surprise, and nothing I enquire will change that outcome. She folds her long-fingered hands, ringless and pale, in her lap and continues her tale.

"In the early 1880s, the British Museum was seeing a

lull in the number of visitors to the Egyptian department. Not many new artifacts had been added to the collection since the museum's founding director, Sir Hans Sloane, acquired his collection of Egyptian antiquities in the early 1800s. And the Museum feared the Egyptians would start to see the value of their own history and become even more demanding and difficult. So, Newton wanted C to significantly develop the museum's relationship with Egypt with regards to excavations."

"Sounds complex," I mumble.

"It was," Catherine agrees. "And it became worse. To make his task as broad as possible – a habit C has, which at times makes him long-winded and slow - he decided to focus on 'scientifically documenting and studying all ancient Egyptian culture,' not only the pyramids. It partly explains why we spent so much time there." Another deep sigh. "Are you sure you want to hear all this? Oh! We need to get back to De Crillon to catch our carriage."

"We have time," I say soothingly. "Plenty of time for you to tell me your story. When do you expect us to be in Cairo? It's the 21st of May today."

Catherine seems to be calculating in her head. It must be incredible to have made this journey so often that you know what to expect without a diary or train schedule to hand.

"Mid-June. Before the heatwave, hopefully," she grins. "But don't worry. The Shepheard's Hotel is the coolest place in all Cairo, and sitting in the shade in the garden with a lemon sherbet is heavenly."

"I can't wait to see it with my own eyes," I say. And I actually mean it.

We slowly make out way back through the Jardin and before I know it, we're on the train to Marseille. I'm spellbound.

7

THE LIFE OF A TRAVELLING LADY

The Night Train to Marseille, later that night, 21-22 May 1896

After Catherine's disclosure of her ties to Egypt during our walk in the Jardin de Tuileries, we seem to settle into companionable travellers, which gives me a feeling of ease. The further the distance between Honeydew Mansion and me, the lighter I start to feel. Anticipation and excitement are beginning to replace worry and doubt.

I'm not sure travelling agrees with my aging dog, though. Jasper keeps up a perky spirit and wags his tail at every stranger, but he sleeps whenever we sit down. It's a comfort the tiredness doesn't affect his appetite. He finishes the French sausages and pork chops I feed him down to the last morsel.

We're now settling for the night in our private compartment, en route to the Port of Marseille. I still can't believe I'm doing this, but the reality of this trip no longer impairs me. I like the rocking of the train carriage beneath my feet, the excitement of the unknown ahead, the lifting of gloom from my heart thanks to all the new experiences. At least for now, I surrender to it. I may come to regret this.

Two unchaperoned ladies on an unorthodox, unsure - maybe even unsafe! - journey to the sands of Africa! Here we are lying in nightdresses and caps in narrow, yet comfortably swaying, berths, chatting amiable. Without any further probing on my part, Catherine has continued her Egypt tale as we lie in the dim light of a single lamp with the rattling train wheels below us. Sure enough, if she can palaver about her beloved C, and she's found willing ears in me, she's as happy as a foal in a spring meadow.

"Within a year C managed to revolutionize the field of Egyptology with his meticulous attention to detail and his emphasis on recording context and stratigraphy," Catherine lectures in a proud voice. The lulling movement of the carriage and Jasper's warm body next to me on the quilt make me drowsy, but I do my best to concentrate on my cousin's words.

"Since being in Egypt, C has introduced a wide array of new methods and techniques in archaeological fieldwork. Renowned archaeologists all over the globe make use of these now."

"Did you also manage to bring new artifacts back to England?" I ask, before a digression into archaeological operations will surely make me fall asleep and vex Catherine.

"Oh yes!" she cries out enthusiastically. "Did you not visit the British Museum in recent years?"

"I didn't," I admit, not adding that I've never even set foot in the Museum's Egyptian collection. I'm more suited to the history of fashion and domestic life. But I keep my tongue.

"C and I shipped off everything personally from Alexandria, just to be sure. I mean, we didn't carry the crates ourselves, as they were way too heavy, but we oversaw the packing and loading and embarked on the vessel that transported them. We didn't leave our treasures out of our sight for even a moment."

Suddenly I remember an article in The Cotswolds Times praising the brand-new Egyptian collection in London. An announcement I scanned at the time with little interest. It never even dawned on me my cousin may had been involved in such important transactions!

"The collection included objects from different pyramid complexes, not just from the Great Pyramid of Khufu," Catherine explains. "Statues, reliefs, funerary items, and everyday objects. Our most important trophies were the granite sarcophagus of King Amenemhat III from Hawara, the limestone false door of Ptahshepses from Saqqara, and the colossal statue of King Ramesses II from the Ramesseum."

Now I am in awe. Totally.

"*You* did that, Catherine? That's a class all by itself." But she shrugs off my admiration.

"It wasn't me. It was C. I was just there to keep him 'sane and sound', as he used to say. And I tried to do just that. These were crazy times, Immy, crazy times."

I try to imagine my slender, upper-class cousin checking boxes in exotic ports with a sun hat on her head and notepad and pen in hand.

"C also managed to smooth some ruffled feathers between the Egyptian and British authorities and institutions on various archaeological projects. He organized joint excavations and research initiatives between the British Museum and Egyptian archaeologists. This way the Egyptians were able to expand their knowledge about their own ancient history and the pyramids. They learnt, or perhaps one ought to say 'relearnt', their own history, art, and religious practices."

"But do the Egyptians accept British dominance over the excavations and ownership claims over items of their own history?" It seems odd to me.

"Not all Egyptian archaeologists are happy with the British interference, if that's what you mean," Catherine replies moodily. Her remark is followed by that sigh I've come to interpret as 'there's some trouble in Egypt'.

"And how did you and C handle that?" I venture to ask.

"Not," is the curt reply. "C was called back to England last year. And he went back to his wife."

"Oh, how sad."

"I'm tired, Immy. I'll explain more tomorrow. Let us sleep."

"Yes," I agree, "and please know you can confide in me, Cathy. Being a constable's wife has had its advantages. I'm good at keeping my mouth shut when I'm not supposed to say anything." And with that, I slip into the pet name I used to call her as a child.

"That's good to know, Immy. That's good to know."

I lay awake thinking about my cousin and her life. In a matter of day, she's become the centre of my life. I should have expected it, but I didn't.

8

BRINDISI

Brindisi, Italy, a week later, 29 May 1896

It is a vibrant and sunny day in late May when Catherine and I arrive in the bustling port city of Brindisi on the south-eastern coast of Italy. The trip through France and Italy has been calm and uneventful, which did us both good. I needed to settle into a travelling spirit and Catherine seemed quite agitated after her last remarks on C.'s return to England and his reunion with his wife.

We left it at that. I'm quite at ease with our adventure now. I don't believe I'll be hauling cases stuffed with mummies or ancient bric-a-brac back to England for our return. Even Jasper seems to have resigned himself to no longer chasing rabbits around Tiversack Lake. He sleeps, he eats and seems happy enough, wagging his tail at strangers and getting many a pat on the head. Yes, it's doing us both good to be away from England for the present.

As I don't think I personally have anything to worry about regarding Egypt, I'll make sure to keep an eye on Catherine. It's not like she's in any danger as far as I can see. She said only C was officially involved in the excavations and transports. But I'm getting ahead of myself, as usual. We're in Italy. Much further south than I've ever been. The only time I have previously been to Italy was in 1864, when Thaddeus and I went to Florence and Venice on our honeymoon.

Brindisi is a lively, nautical port city. Already quite far south with a dry and tropical nature, my surroundings were mostly decked in pale grey-greens and the azure of the Mediterranean. A far cry from the green, rainy hills of the Cotswolds and the dark, choppy waters of Tiversack Lake.

The atmosphere is filled with the scents of sea salt and distant lands. The sun, high in the sky, casts golden rays upon the lively streets, painting the facades of colourful buildings in warm hues of ochre and terracotta.

Catherine and I have taken up residence in Grand Hotel Brindisi, a luxury hotel she has stayed at before. And we're not the only foreigners.

"It's the only decent hotel in Brindisi that accommodates tourists and provides comfortable lodging and services. Some of the staff even speaks broken English," Catherine had announced.

We're sitting at the breakfast table overlooking the waterfront. Breakfast is something of a feast here that even challenges my reluctant appetite.

"Are you used to drinking coffee with your breakfast, Cathy, after all your travelling?" I ask as I see her pour us two steaming cups without a second thought.

"Oh, yes. You'd better forget all about tea. At least until we're at the Shepheard's. There are so many Brits there, they simply must have a large storage of English Breakfast on-hand, or a riot would break out. I've known of travellers who bring their own tea along. One man took his bag of tea right into the Borneo jungle. Didn't have much use for it, though! I don't bother. I drink what I'm offered. Did you bring your own tea?"

"I didn't even give it a second thought," I reply. "but I'll be glad to sip a cup of tea when we finally arrive at our destination. So yes, I do miss it." But as I taste the sweetened, black liquid from the small espresso cup, I must agree it's good. And its strength peps me up in seconds.

"You could have the hot chocolate instead?" Catherine suggests, pointing to the jug of hot milk and chocolate powder on the silver tray. I shake my head, "I'm fine with coffee."

Next come the breads. There are so many different kinds. Ciabatta, pane di Genzano, focaccia. I mean who can eat all that for breakfast? Jasper doesn't protest. He munches them all with pleasure. Then there are also pastries, brioche, and a kind of sweet roll. I nibble off a corner of each one and share the rest with Jasper. They are all delicious. Catherine spreads hers thick with butter and apricot jam. That girl has an appetite. I don't understand how she stays so slim.

"It is a lot, but it's good, isn't it?" Catherine voices while she licks away the last crumbs from her lips. "You simply must try those biscotti, or cantuccini."

"I can't. Honestly. I'll just have some of those juicy grapes." Fresh fruits are aplenty as well - oranges, grapes, and apples, all vibrantly coloured by hours of sunlight.

I drink my second cup of coffee while Catherine serves herself a variety of cheeses and cured meats, which she labels ricotta, pecorino, prosciutto, salami."

"Hmmm," she finishes off her copious breakfast grinning like a Cheshire cat. "That's why I like Italy. I could live here for the food."

"I'm so full I think I'll burst!" I laugh. "But you're right, I haven't had a breakfast like this all my life. It's a feast for kings."

"Queens!" Catherine corrects me and I nod, feeling such a strong bond with her, as if we're both young and playful again. As if life didn't happen, didn't come in between us.

"You'd better stuff yourself well these next days, Immy," Catherine advises, "crossing the Mediterranean is no sinecure. You with your lack of sea legs better make sure you have some reserves."

"Don't spoil a perfect day with what's to come," I grumble mockingly.

"You've been warned!" She wags a long finger at me.

We have three days before we board the SS Karnak, the steamship that will take us all the way to Alexandria.

As two eager land-travellers arriving at the waterfront, we find ourselves immersed in the bustling scene of maritime activity after breakfast. The harbour teems with an eclectic mix of ships and vessels, their sails billowing in the gentle coastal breeze. Tanned sailors in nautical attire hustle and bustle around the docks, their voices intermingling with the sounds of creaking wood and seagulls screaming overhead.

Stepping onto the quay, we're greeted by a symphony of sights and sounds that tell tales of distant lands and exotic adventures. Market stalls adorned with vibrant awnings line the waterfront, showcasing an array of tantalizing goods from all corners of the world. Fragrant spices, glistening silks, and intricately woven carpets create a kaleidoscope of colours that beckon the curious eyes of passers-by.

I put my arm through Catherine's, partly to be close to her but also so as not to lose sight of her. It is so busy and chaotic around us.

I listen to the medley of languages dancing through the air, as merchants and locals engage in animated conversations, their voices resonating with excitement and anticipation. Italian, Arabic, French, and English intertwine, forming a harmonious linguistic tapestry that reflects the cosmopolitan nature of this bustling hub of trade and travel.

My attention is drawn to the magnificent ferry anchored at the pier, a true marvel of engineering and elegance. Its towering smokestacks exhale gentle puffs of smoke, hinting at the power that will soon propel us across the vast expanse of the Mediterranean. The vessel's polished brass fittings glimmer in the sunlight, while the gentle clanking of chains and creaking ropes create a melodic rhythm that lingers in the air.

"Is that the SS Karnak?" I ask surprised, having not expected the boat to already be in the harbour.

"It is," Catherine affirms, "It must just have returned from Alexandria. The ship is owned and operated by the Peninsular and Oriental Steam Navigation Company. Did you know?"

"Oh, the same as between Dover and Calais, and through the Suez Canal." I'm still admiring the huge vessel. It looks much sturdier and bigger than the ferries through the English Channel.

The heat is starting to be oppressive and Jasper lags behind.

"Let's sit down at this quaint café," Catherine suggests. I agree, as its outdoor terrace adorned with wrought iron furniture looks inviting. We settle ourselves at a small table and savour another cup of the richly scented, freshly brewed coffee, its fragrance mingling with the salty sea breeze. As we sip our drinks, I'm absorbing the energetic ambiance around me and I feel the pulse of adventure and discovery that permeates every corner of Brindisi's historic port. And now, of my own heart.

"I can't wait for that ferry's horn to sound and start our voyage to Alexandria, Cathy. Thank you for inviting me."

"I'm happy you're happy," Catherine squeezes my hand. Even the shadow that glides over her face can't stop my happiness.

I feel like my eyes are shining and my heart overflows. The ship is like the promise of a new horizon, an unknown land, gateway to a world awaiting exploration.

9

SEEING EGYPT FOR THE FIRST TIME

Alexandria, two weeks later, 12 June 1896

As the sun cast its golden glow over the bustling streets of Alexandria, Catherine, Jasper, and I emerge from the marble-clad entrance of the luxurious Hotel Cecil. We've been staying in Alexandria for three days to recuperate from our sea voyage across the Mediterranean. Let me just look back on these days and remark, "they weren't too bad, but they certainly weren't the best days of my life."

It wasn't just seasickness that put a brake on the optimism I'd felt in Brindisi, it was also Catherine's fidgetiness. She snapped at me a couple of times and when I asked what was bothering her, she said it was nothing, "just the heat." But I doubted it. For some reason she seems to dread arriving in Cairo. Maybe it's because of the fond memories she has of the place with her C, maybe it's something else altogether.

"Let's just enjoy our last day here," I suggest, taking

her arm as usual. So far Alexandria has been sweltering hot, but interesting in a different way. Paris was sweet and romantic; Brindisi was copious and abuzz like the London horse bus on a summer Sunday. The soul of Alexandria I have not yet probed, so I'll stick with interesting for now.

With our parasols up and dressed in our finest gowns, we set out on foot to the local bazaar. I've hired a young and strong Egyptian called Mahmoud to carry Jasper for me. It's way too hot to let my poor Roly-Poly walk. The dark-haired Mahmoud follows on our heels and Jasper seems comfortable, now and then licking the sweat trickling from the man's jaw, which makes Mahmoud laugh out loud.

Catherine looks particularly stunning today. Her soft yellow gown is adorned with a touch of delicate lace and vibrant silk.

Just to perk her up, I compliment her on her radiant looks. I'm glad to see a smile slide across her face.

"I like dressing up in Egypt more than in England. Never have to worry about ruining your skirts with mud and rain here."

"Duly noted," I say, "I'm glad then that I brought my best summer gowns."

I'm aware the two of us must be exuding an air of mystery and intrigue that sets us apart from the other tourists. Two British ladies on their own is not a familiar sight in Egypt. This became clear to me from the moment we docked in the harbour of Alexandria. The looks men gave us and the diverted gazes from the heavily veiled women. Where Italy had a certain freedom and acceptance, this Islamic country has different rules when it comes to women.

"No need for us to adapt, Immy. Unless we enter a mosque. Just dress as you would in England, dear," Catherine had answered on my question whether I should wear a veil around my hat to cover my face.

With undeniable grace and poise, as the British tend to demonstrate abroad, Catherine with a straw-hat on her wavy blonde hair, framing a face that holds her enigmatic smile, leads the way in an energetic pace. I follow where she directs me, not letting go of her arm. Now and then the green eyes dart to mine. Hers have a sparkle today that's new but also a hint of a secret she holds close. In spite of her peppy spirit, I feel less exuberant, and even slightly bewildered today. Though I'm still curious what Cairo will hold for us, Catherine's temperamentality is hard for me to follow.

We walk along the Canopic Way, one of Alexandria's ancient's streets that connects the city's eastern and western parts. Shaded by the canopies from which it derives its name, the street's tapestry of sights, sounds, and aromas engulfs me. The air is full of spices, incense, and a tinge of sea salt wafting in from the nearby harbour. Soon we find ourselves immersed in the exotic charm of a busy bazaar, a blend of cultures, colours, and commerce. I don't know where to look, there is so much. Catherine seems to enjoy my enchantment.

"Never seen anything like this at the Landdulton church bazaar, have you?" she giggles.

"Never," I say. "Thank you for bringing me, Cathy. It's a feast for the eyes." Yet, I'm also aware it's a haven for pickpockets and small criminals, making me a bit anxious.

The streets are narrow and winding, lined with buildings from architectural influences unfamiliar to me. The facades are painted in vibrant colours, intricate tile patterns catch my eye, reflecting the cultural mosaic that defines this cosmopolitan city.

As we venture farther, the lively sounds of haggling, merchants' calls, and the rhythmic clatter of horse-drawn carriages fill the air. The crowd is a kaleidoscope of diversity, with locals donning traditional Egyptian garments, Bedouins in their flowing robes, and Europeans in their formal attire. The medley of languages spoken - from Arabic to French to English - creates a symphony of voices that harmoniously blends in the air.

Stalls and shops line the labyrinthine alleyways, each one brimming with treasures and trinkets from distant lands. Silk fabrics from India hang in vibrant hues, their patterns intricately woven. Piles of spices from the East release an intoxicating aroma, tempting passers-by with their exotic flavours. I can almost taste the richness of cinnamon, cloves, and cardamom that permeate the atmosphere.

As Catherine and I meander through the labyrinthine paths, still with Mahmoud carrying Jasper on our heels, we pass stalls laden with carpets, in beautiful colours and intricate designs. Behind the stalls, craftsmen deftly weave the threads of different colours, creating their geometric patterns and floral motifs. Craftsmanship, no doubt passed down through generations.

"I understand why you fell in love with this country," I say. "It's amazing."

Catherine gives my arm a sudden jerk, which makes me stop in my tracks and causes Mahmoud to almost bump into us. The green eyes are a flash with anger. "Did I ever – I mean e-v-e-r – say I loved this country? I loathe it!"

"Catherine!" I cry out, vexed and mortified. "What do you mean? Why did you bring me here if you hate it so?" The light in her eyes softens. Then she kisses my cheek, light and breezy and smiles again. "Sorry, that was crass! I shouldn't have said that. My mind was on C. The last time we were here together, he bought me this necklace." She points to the golden chain around her neck. "I don't hate Egypt. I hate and love it. If that's possible. But right now, you're right, I love it. Let's have oriental tea."

After Catherine's outburst, I've become overwhelmed. The bazaar is a sensory overload for me - all the colourful textiles, brass lanterns, and shimmering gold jewellery. The sounds of men hammering metals and woodworkers carving designs mingle with the laughter and banter of the shoppers, creating a din that makes it impossible to focus. It is hot and I'm confused.

After tea, the air finally seems to cool, and Catherine looks calm and happy. I personally can't wait to get to Cairo and be at our destination. Though the Alexandria bazaar is an unforgettable experience, I'm ready to be done with travelling for a while, and long for a longer stay at the Shepheard's Hotel. With a degree of English-ness, I can't deny thinking.

~

As we step onto the platform of the ornate Alexandria train station, the steam-powered locomotive stands waiting for us, all polished brass and gleaming wood. Suddenly a loud call to prayer fills the air, rising above the buzz at the station. Not the familiar sound of St Mary's Church bell calling us to Evening Mass but a strange, long-drawn singsong voice reciting from the top of a minaret. It sounds melancholic and foreign. It makes me realize how far away from home I am. I sigh deeply as we board, tiredness in my limbs.

"How many hours to Cairo?" I ask as we're settled in our compartment and Jasper is comfortable as well.

"Five to six hours," Catherine replies, taking off her hat and shaking her blonde hair loose. "We should be there before midnight."

"How do we get to the hotel?" I try not to panic, envisioning us traipsing through Cairo in the black, desert night.

"Don't worry. There will be several carriages waiting at the station. This train always brings foreigners to Cairo that need to go to Shepheard's."

"Oh." My relief is great and after the long day, I shut my eyes.

As the train rattles along the iron tracks, I doze for what feels like a brief moment and then wake. Catherine seems to be fast asleep and so is Jasper. My darling is even snoring. I must have actually slept for a spell because the light is fading fast in the rapidly approaching evening hour.

Outside my window are vast stretches of golden sand dunes rolled like waves under the setting sun, while palm trees sway in the distance, as if whispering secrets only they know. Our windows are lined with elegant lace curtains that move with the rhythm of the train, casting long shadows on the polished wood panelling.

We pass sleepy villages and dust-ridden paths into nowhere. Now and then, a fellow traveller passes in the corridor, most of them Europeans. A weary explorer in khaki outfit, his clothes caked with red desert dust; an enigmatic figure hidden in a black cape; someone I'm sure must be a scholar, carrying a stack of weathered manuscripts. I wonder if I'll see any of them again at the hotel in Cairo. After all, Catherine said it was *the* place to stay for Europeans.

While the light fades obscuring the view out the window, I let my gaze wander to my sleeping cousin opposite me. She is slouched in her chair with the long limbs stretched out, a hand nestling against her fair cheek.

"Who are you?" I ask in the dusk. "What is it you really need me here for?" But I promised her that I will try to help her. As long as it's nothing illegal. That will be my line in the sand, and I will not cross it.

As the train finally screeches to a halt in Cairo, Catherine yawns, stretches and opens her eyes.

"Ah, we're here. I had the weirdest dream just now. I'll tell you when we're at the hotel."

10

THE SHEPHEARD'S HOTEL

Shepheard's Hotel, Cairo, the same evening, 12 June 1896

Our driver drops us off with all our luggage and a frazzled Jasper in the very heart of Cairo, where Shepheard's Hotel stands majestically on the banks of the Nile River. Though it is dark, the hotel and its surroundings are lit up by gas lamps that reflect on the surface of the ink-black water and show the sprawled contours of the four-storeyed hotel.

Two Egyptian footmen, dressed in European suits and with white gloves, hasten down the steps to help us descend from the carriage and load our luggage on a waiting trolley. Despite my tiredness, I stand and look around, awe-filled.

"It's breath-taking. Even at night with the view over the river mostly hidden, the hotel, the cityscape, everything. Who'd have thought."

"Over there is the Egyptian Museum and there the

Khan el-Khalili bazaar. Both very interesting landmarks that we will visit in due time." Catherine points left and right as a proud guide. She looks radiant in the midnight air and seems highly relieved we have arrived. So am I.

"We'll start exploring the wonders of Cairo tomorrow," she adds. "But bed and bath now. And perhaps a late-night snack, as we didn't really have much on the train."

I am happy to agree. It's the first time I truly feel like a tourist. The luxury and prestige of this hotel makes me feel like an affluent and well-travelled client, which Catherine may be, but I certainly am not.

As we enter the hotel, I'm both impressed and surprised. Who would have guessed that a prototype of Victorian architecture would have been erected in Egypt? Though I spot some Oriental design elements here and there. The exterior boasts ornate facades, intricate carvings, arches, and balconies, the interior is opulent, with lavish furnishings, chandeliers, and marble floors. Definitely a place for the rich and famous.

It looks like my cousin is one of those, because an important looking man with black hair and an enormous black moustache heaves his bulky body from a chair and comes towards us.

"Mrs Northwind, what a pleasure!" the big man exclaims with what sounds like a German accent. He jovially shakes Catherine hands and then mine.

"Glad to be back under your wings, Mr Zech. But you needn't have stayed up for us." Catherine secretly seems to enjoy the hotelier's special favour. "This my cousin, Mrs Imogene Lynch. Please treat her with care as it's her first time here in Cairo.'

"Don't we always treat everyone as if they're Wedgwood china, Mrs Northwind? Welcome Mrs Lynch. I hope you will enjoy your stay with us."

"Have you prepared the usual rooms, Mr Zech?"

"Need you even ask, Mrs Northwind?"

Catherine and I are escorted to the second floor by the jovial hotelier himself and led to our ensuite rooms. My quarters include two spacious rooms - a sitting room and a bedroom - tastefully decorated with Victorian-era furniture and tapestries, with water colours of Egyptian landscapes on the walls. They create an ambiance of comfort and elegance. I peeked through the closed curtains to guarantee myself I'll have a panoramic view of the Nile River in the morning.

For now, I say goodnight to Catherine and Jasper, and I sink in a deep, pleasant sleep. In the far distance are the sounds of the city and the occasional ship's horn on the river.

I wake startled by a soft knock on my door. Quickly rising to a sitting position, I gaze around me in complete darkness and wonder where I am.

"Madam, would you like to dine in your room, or will you come down to the breakfast room?" a British voice enquires from the corridor.

Cairo. I'm in Cairo. In the Shepheard's Hotel. Now I remember. Next to me my darling Jasper stirs in his sleep. For the first night, I've given in to allow him to sleep on the bed.

"Uh...I'll come down, thank you." I call back as I

wonder what time it is. As the room is shrouded in dark-ness, with the thick curtains closed, I suppose it's past sunrise, but I slip out of bed and tug one curtain open. Incredibly bright sunlight blinds me for a moment, and I realize it must be later than I expected. My watch says it's 9:30am. I feel dazed and late.

Will Catherine have gone down already without waking me? I listen at the door between us but there's no sound. I call out to her. No answer. Dithering a moment between waiting for her and going downstairs before it's too late for breakfast, I decide to slip a note under her door.

I dress as quickly and as excursion worthy as I can. My dresses are crumpled from having been in their valises for weeks. I'll have to ask the hotel staff to have them pressed and aired today.

"Come on, darling, time for breakfast." The word 'break-fast' does its usual trick and Jasper gets up on the bed, stretches his arthritic limbs and yawns extensively. A long red tongue hangs out from between yellowish teeth. He looks like he is grinning, and that always makes me glad. Despite the long journey, my Roly-Poly looks well. He even jumps off the bed himself and lands without sinking through his leggies.

"Time for an adventure," I announce, and he wags his tail.

11

THE HERRIOTS ARE HERE

The Shepheard's Hotel breakfast room, the same day, 13 June 1896

The breakfast room is empty but for one elderly couple sitting in a corner sipping their after-breakfast coffee. They seem British to me, giving a curt nod in my direction, before continuing their conversation in hushed tones. Unsure about customs among tourists here, I nod back but don't introduce myself.

No sight of Catherine. I choose a table for Jasper and myself at one of the bay windows overlooking the Nile River. The glittering water basks in the late morning sun. Ships of all shapes and sizes glide past, practically beneath our window. The Nile is almost busier than the Thames, certainly more chaotic.

A waiter hastens my way to help me with my chair.

"Are you Mrs Lynch?" he asks in English with a thick accent I assume is Arabic.

"Yes, I am. Sorry I'm late for breakfast."

"Not late at all, Madam. But there's a note for you from Mrs Northwind. Let me fetch it for you."

A note from Catherine? For a second the panicky thought grips me she has abandoned me to go off on her own. Snatching the envelope from the silver tray the waiter presents to me, I see it is indeed in Catherine's distinctive handwriting. As distinctive as she is herself. I rip open the scented envelope to read.

> Dear Immy,
> I was up early and went for a walk and an errand. Had breakfast upstairs.
> I will be back in an hour.
> Yours Catherine

THOUGH I FIND this slightly odd, I am glad to be told she'll be back.

"Would you like a Continental or an English breakfast, Mrs Lynch?"

Though English will be heavy on the stomach, I don't trust the Continental option.

"I'll have the English. And the sausages well cooked, please. And an extra plate for my dog."

"Of course, Madam."

While waiting for the arrival of our food, I inspect the room. It's as impressive and opulent as the rest of the hotel. It is as if the best of British design has been brought to the heart of Cairo. It makes me wonder who Mr Shepheard, the creator of all this wealth away from home, really is. I must ask Catherine.

I try to remember an article from back home about the hotel's change of hands years ago, which I didn't pay much attention to. But my benedict always said I had the memory of an elephant. If I need the details, they pop right back in my brain.

So, if I remember correctly, the article said Samuel Shepheard co-owned the hotel in the 1840s with a friend who was the head coachman of a rich Egyptian. Can you imagine? That must have been a coachman with more aplomb than my grumpy driver, Tomas Rand. The article described Mr Shepheard as a remarkable man in many ways, the model *John Bull*.

But he sold the hotel in 1861 to a Bavarian hotelier and retired back to England. The current owner must be the Mr Zech who welcomed us last night.

Sitting here amidst so many things that I love about Britain while abroad, I'm actually grateful for having some time alone with Jasper. My poor Roly-Poly has been neglected somewhat by all my attention going to Catherine during our journey.

He so enjoys the little morsels of bacon and sausages I feed him. They are well-cooked so his stomach will not play up. How he looks up at me with his velvety brown eyes as if he wants to say, "life in Egypt isn't too bad, is it, Mistress?"

I must agree. I enjoy my excellent cup of Ceylon tea after all the strong and black cups of coffee on the European Continent. And the toast and beans taste just like at home.

At that moment the breakfast door opens, and an elegant couple walk in. No doubt about their Britishness!

I force myself not to let my jaw drop in surprise. It can't be true, but it is. It's Mr and Mrs Herriot from Dartmond, the hoity-toity industrialist who owns the lavender mills and soap factory and his dressed-to-the-nines wife. What are they doing here?

But then I remember Catherine told me this hotel is *the place to be* for British aristocracy *and* those with 'new money'.

I'm not sure they've recognized me, as our paths didn't really cross during my year in Dartmond to solve the mystery of the secret Christmas baby. You remember, finding out who my cousin Finley's birth mother was. Gosh that seems ages ago now. But it brought Catherine, on paper Finley's sister, back into my orbit.

The Herriots don't give a sign of recognition as they take a table at the other side of the breakfast room. Just as well. There will, hopefully, be plenty agreeable Brits to chat with in that famous Shepheard's terrace and garden Catherine mentioned. Still, I can't keep myself from studying the couple. I've only seen them through a window before, when they would pass the Hopewell's book shop and I could peer down from my cramped apartment on Darren Street.

They look not as pompous as I remember -Ralph puffing out his chest like the chief peacock and Winnifred swirling like a cloud of lace and lavender by his side. Maybe they have just arrived and are still travel-weary, or they keep that I-own-the-place attitude for when they're at home in Dartmond. They don't seem to be communicating much. Ralph is hidden behind The

Times as if he's at home with his pipe and slippers and Winnifred gazes out over the river with an almost skittish look on her face.

I discern all these little details because I love studying people and my years as Thaddeus's second pair of eyes has made me more aware of people's body language and interaction. It's none of my business, of course, but this doesn't come across as a happy couple on an exciting vacation in exotic Egypt. I guess they could be here on business. Or they could just be having a bad morning. It really is none of my business, so I get up to take Jasper for a short stroll in the garden before returning to my room and to wait for Catherine's return.

"Come on Jasper," I urge my darling, who's still licking his plate as if he wants to scrape off the glazing.

When I pass the Herriot's table, Winnifred looks up and greets me with a curt nod. The nod says she does recognize me but isn't interested in a chat. Well, neither am I, so I nod and turn my back on them.

12

A LAST DAY OF LEISURE

Cairo, later the same day, 13 June 1896

Catherine looks flustered and hot when she comes into my room just before midday. And her voice is a tad too chirpy.

"Oh darling, you're up. Have you had breakfast? It's so hot outside, I think we must only have a short excursion today. Maybe the mosque. Nice and cool."

I watch her perch on the arm of a chair, light as a sparrow, as if ready to flutter out of the window and out of sight. It lies on the tip of my tongue to ask her if something is the matter, but the green eyes warn me not to ask questions.

"You'd better leave Jasper behind. The poor thing will melt in the street. I'm sure there's someone in the hotel who can look after him. Are you ready to explore, Immy?"

I rise to collect my parasol and summer coat.

"No need to bring a coat, darling. Just a shawl to veil

your face if we're visiting the mosque. It's way too hot for a coat."

Catherine's high-pitched voice is exasperating and irritating to my ears, but I still say nothing. I understand she is recovering from something that happened to her that morning and she will tell me in due time. Or not. Which can always be the case with my clouded cousin.

"Let's go then," I say in what I hope is an enthusiastic enough voice. "Unless you want a refreshment before you dash out again?"

"No, no need. We'll have a coffee and a sherbet in town. I'm fine. Really, I'm fine."

"I'm not leaving Jasper here on his own. I need to see if there is a possibility to let him stay behind in the hotel with someone to watch him."

"The staff will look after him, don't worry," Catherine says with confidence. "I've seen so many people from home leave their dogs in the kennel in the garden. They're used to it here at Shepheard's."

AN HOUR later we step out of a carriage pulled by two sweaty black horses and driven by a driver even sulkier than my Tomas. After a bit of a haggle between him and Catherine over his exorbitant price for such a short ride, we step onto one of Cairo's dusty and busy streets.

My eyes widen in awe as I take in all the vibrance and colours of this ancient city unrolling before me in the bright midday sun. I draw in all the scents I am still getting accustomed to: the fragrant ingredients of the traditional Egyptian cuisine, cumin, coriander, mint, and garlic, the smell of markets stalls selling fruits and flowers.

Catherine, a much more seasoned traveller than me, seems unperturbed by the grandeur and mystique around her and continues to grumble over the penny-pinching driver.

"Let it go, Cathy," I soothe her. "It's unimportant. Let's enjoy our exploration of the City of a Thousand Minarets."

"You're right. I didn't sleep well and then I let these locals get under my skin. I should know better by now." Catherine hooks her arm through mine and directs us towards what she calls 'the famous Khan el-Khalili Market.'

We make slow progress. The streets are incredibly busy and full, not just with people but carts and donkeys and children and dogs. The intense heat washing over us also hampers our progress.

Though we can protect our fair skin from the direct sunlight with parasols and gloves, we cannot escape the heat. Scorching as I've never felt it before, the rays of the sun beat down on us relentlessly. They reflect off the white-washed buildings and sand-covered pavements, almost blinding me. I pull my hat as far as possible over my eyes but so that I can still see where to place my feet.

Even though I dressed in my lightest linen gown, my underskirts and corset make me feel as if I've still got too many layers on. I constantly fan myself with my lace handkerchief, to little avail. Catherine seems unfazed by the temperature. She guides me through the city streets, pointing out architectural wonders visible above the moving crowds. I wish I could see more of the beautifully designed mosques with their minarets reaching towards the sky, but that requires me to look up and into the sun, and it is quite impossible to open one's eyes into such bright sunlight. Instead, I focus on the vibrant bazaars in front of me, filled with exotic spices and trinkets, and the lush gardens with their blooming flowers.

We finally arrive at the Khan el-Khalili Market, which is a labyrinth of narrow alleyways filled with merchants hawking their wares. Here too, the air is filled with the aroma of spices and the noise of lively bargaining is almost deafening. I feel my senses stretched to their limits with all the overwhelming sensations. It's a good thing we didn't bring Jasper. It's altogether too much for an elderly human, let alone for an old dog.

"Let's find a place to sit down and have lunch," Catherine suggests, and I welcome the idea as a call to paradise.

Seeking respite from the relentless sun, we retreat to a traditional teahouse tucked away in a quiet corner of the market. Inside, the coolness of the shaded courtyard provides a much-needed relief from the heat outside. We sit on ornately cushioned divans, sipping sweet, mint tea. Catherine strikes up an animated conversation with some local shopkeepers and I'm surprised to learn she speaks Arabic. There are so many wonders about my cousin. I'm just happy to sit in the shade and wouldn't have said no to a quick nap. The heat is draining me of energy.

I listen to Catherine talk in her singsong voice and my head starts to nod. Then I'm suddenly wide awake and shocked. With the clarity of water in a mountain stream I know Catherine's ulterior motive to be in Egypt now. She hopes to reunite with C. For some reason she knows he's here and she's looking for him.

I study my cousin's profile and wonder more about her. And about her secrets. Should I tell her I know? But what purpose would it serve? None. I keep quiet, wondering what happens if she finds him, whether she'll introduce him to me or just have secret rendezvous leaving me to believe her private excursions are about visiting friends from earlier trips.

I do wonder why she let me follow on her coat tails. Does she need me for some reason, or as emotional support if the reunion fails?

Fie, Imogene, I scold myself, *don't think so badly of your poor cousin. Her heart is broken, and she can't let him go. Wouldn't you have done everything in your power to keep Thaddeus at your side? Love is love, whatever form it takes.*

"You're mighty quiet, Immy. And that look on your face tells me you're on to something. Will you share?" Catherine turns away from her new friends and returns to speaking English. I had overlooked the obvious. She is smart as a whip and knows me inside and out, since we were children. Didn't she tell me I'm an open book?

"It's nothing," I say quickly. "I just want you to be happy."

"Oh, but I am happy now, dear Immy. Isn't it lovely to be sitting here together in the shade, sipping tea? Thank you for coming with me." She kisses my cheek all of sudden with that characteristic warmth of hers and turns back to her conversation with the Egyptians.

I don't tell her this is more proof she's up to something that's got little to do with me.

Catherine takes leave of her new acquaintances and focuses her attention on me once again.

"As it's such a hot day, let us sit here in the teahouse for the present. I'd planned for us to spend the whole day in the city centre, but I don't want to wear you out on day one. It's exceptionally hot, even to Cairo standards. But I wouldn't forgive myself if you hadn't at least heard the momentous sounds of the call to prayer from these quarters once, and today is as good as any. We're surrounded by minarets, as you've seen. The *adhan* is a call to God – or Allah I should say – as much as it's a call to his worshippers. You heard it in Alexandria, right? Well, it's that but then augmented tenfold. Here it tickles the eardrums until they almost burst."

"I'm not sure you're making it sound very enticing, Cathy," I smile. She looks at me with a serious frown.

"The *adhan* isn't enticing. It's melancholic and soul-rending."

"You're not ... converted...are you, Catherine?" My voice almost falters. That would be just the thing for her!

"Heavens, no! What do you take me for? I'm still as Church of England as... well as I'm supposed to be." The green eyes are full of mischief.

"You shouldn't make jokes about the Faith, cousin." I can't help sounding prim and stern.

"Oh Immy, you're as good as the Lord himself. Don't worry about my soul. I certainly don't intend to end up in an Egyptian sarcophagus if that's what you're thinking."

"Well enough of this serious talk. After we've listened to the call to prayer, we'll go to my favourite spot on the Nile and just gaze out over the water. Then I'll take you to an enchanting belly dancer performance." Her eyes shine and I can see she's as happy as a young lamb again. Who knows what was exchanged in Arabic with these shop-keepers? Oh, I'm like a hound when I'm on a trail!

"I don't know about belly dancers," I say doubtful. "Aren't they supposed to show their naked waists?"

Women showing their naked bellies may be part and parcel of the culture, I'm not sure it meets my Church of England standards.

"Oh, it's all very decent, Immy. Don't worry. We will only be allowed to the shows that accept foreigners. No belly buttons visible, I promise." Catherine giggles. "Listen? It's starting. Let's go outside and listen."

I was dragged outside by Catherine's decisive hand with my mind wandering back to Jasper. He was going to be alone at the hotel way too long. I have to tell Catherine that the belly dancers must wait until another day.

"Hayya 'ala-salah" means come to prayer, Catherine translates and "Hayya 'ala-l-falah" means come to success." She translates the entire recital from the muezzin for me and I agree it sounds melancholic and soul-rending but I'm glad when it ends. It's also rather loud and overbearing.

As the day draws to a close, we make our way to the edge of the city centre to witness the sun set over the Nile. The sky blazes with hues of orange and pink, casting a magical glow over the ancient river. I feel a strange sense of wonder and serenity wash over me as I witness the red sun dip below the horizon, painting the world in shades of gold and then in greys and blacks.

13

MR HERRIOT GOES MISSING

Shepheard's Hotel Breakfast Room, one month later, 13 July 1896

Today is a repetition of the day before and every day before that since we have arrived. A note from Catherine that's she's gone out early and will be back soon. Jasper and I breakfast alone, but an hour earlier than on our first morning, so the breakfast room is quite crowded. Still the same waiter accompanies me to the same table and helps me with my chair.

"English Breakfast again with the sausages well-cooked?" He asks in accented English, and I understand why this hotel is so good. They remember the preferences of their clientele and it makes one feel special and accepted.

"Yes, please," I say as I settle Jasper on his seat. The golden morning sun – another hot day no doubt - spills through the large windows of the breakfast room, displaying a scene for me that could come straight out of a novel. The atmosphere here is created as much by the setting as by the guests.

On my first day, I somehow missed seeing the tapestries on the walls that depict different scenes from ancient Egyptian civilization, nor did I see how high the ceilings are and how beautifully decorated with sculpted reliefs. The golden chandeliers look as if they were lifted straight from Queen Victoria's ballroom. They give the room so much elegance and refinement.

My gaze wanders over the busy breakfast tables, covered in pristine white linen, and laid with delicate china and polished silverware. On this fine day the room hums with animated conversations. The well-dressed ladies and gentlemen seem to revel in exchanging stories of their adventures in this land of pharaohs and pyramids, sharing tales of their adventures not just with their own table partners, but also beyond to the neighbouring tables.

It makes me almost feel like an intruder, as I sit alone with my Roly-Poly. Quick glances are directed towards us, a polite nod here and there but nobody attempts to include me in their conversations.

"Just as well," I think, as I like people watching and am usually quite content being by myself. It would have been different had Thaddeus been here, or even Catherine. By the looks of it most, guests are British tourists, though I hear German and a Slavic language I don't recognize from the tables next to me.

Everyone is dressed in their finest attire, as if they're on a fashion parade, which makes for a great show. The gentlemen sport tailored suits, waistcoats, and bowler hats, and there are a variety of military uniforms as well.

The ladies don flowing gowns, with plenty of lace and silk details. The rustling of their luxury garments mingles with the clinking of teacups and the hubbub of well-bred conversation.

More than once I catch phrases like 'pyramids of Giza', 'ancient temples of Luxor', 'bustling Cairo bazaar'. The room echoes with laughter, mingling accents, and the occasional burst of Arabic spoken by knowledgeable guides accompanying the tourists.

I inhale the aroma of freshly brewed tea and rich Egyptian coffee, complemented by the delicate scents of exotic fruits and pastries. Platters piled high with succulent dates, figs, and pomegranates entice guests to indulge in the flavours of the East. Waiters move swiftly through the room, offering silver trays laden with delicate sandwiches, buttery croissants, and warm scones served with clotted cream and preserves. All this is mingled with the spicy, acrid smoke of cigars and pipes puffed by the gentlemen.

It's a feast for the eyes and Jasper can't stop licking his lips in anticipation. While we wait for our own breakfast to arrive, I momentarily gaze out of the window, still faintly aware of the buzz of voices around me, the scraping of chairs, and the mixture of scents.

From my vantage point, I can catch a glimpse of Cairo's vibrant cityscape beyond the hotel's grand facade. The bustling street below, filled with donkey-drawn carts and horse-drawn carriages. They serve as a constant reminder of the exotic and foreign world I have entered.

After having lived among middle-class shopkeepers and locals for decades, being among the British upper-class throws me back to the distant years of my youth, which is quite touching to me at this moment.

Though my parents were upper middle-class, my father being a general in the Duke of Wellington's army and my mother of modest aristocratic birth, our life in London was more refined than what I became used to in the Cotswolds after my marriage to Thaddeus Lynch, who came from a lower middle-class background. My parents never held it against me that I married below my class, but I can't say they were happy with it either.

"You have to lie in the bed you've made," was one of my mother's favourite sayings. It crosses my mind that Egypt may introduce a new phase in my life with my husband having passed and my aristocratic cousin suddenly asking me to travel with her and mix with these well-to-do travellers from a privileged class.

I don't have any more time pondering my philosophical questions because the breakfast door is flung open in a most uncivilized way and Winnifred Herriot marches in. All red-faced and wide-eyed, she hurries straight to my table. For a moment I panic, thinking something has happened to Catherine, but then she blurts out for all to hear.

"Mr Herriot is missing! You must help me find him!"

All eyes turn to me as I utter a bewildered. "Me? What do I have to do with it?"

My question stops Mrs Herriot in her tracks. Now it is *her* turn to look bewildered.

"You are... you are Mrs Lynch, aren't you?"

"Yes, I am. Mrs Imogene Lynch. But I don't know your husband."

For a moment Winnifred bites her lower lip, looks at

me apprehensively. There's something in her face, just a passing glance, that tells me all this has been planned. But I shrug it off.

She drops her voice to a whisper as she perches on the chair opposite me.

"From reliable sources, I've been told you are very good. And this needs to stay hush-hush, you see. That's why I can't go to the police."

Then why make such a spectacle entering the room, I think but don't say.

"Good at what, may I ask?" I reply, though I already know what she's hinting at.

"You know, solving cases of missing people. In a discrete way." Her blue eyes are hopeful and a tad too innocent.

"What if they don't want to be found?" Better grab the bull by the horns. The tiny smile in the corner of her pretty mouth tells me my words strike a chord, but her voice is all wronged indignation when she splutters.

"Why would my husband not want to be found? But listen, Mrs Lynch, we're wasting precious time. If it's money you want, I have plenty." She waves her lace bag before my nose. What terrible manners this industrialist's wife has. Meanwhile, the waiter arrives with my breakfast. Surprised by my new visitor, he quickly changes tactics.

"Oh, Mrs Herriot it is you. Do you want to change places? You can sit at Mrs Lynch's table if you want."

"No, no, garçon, don't bother. I'm not in the mood to have breakfast. Just bring me a black coffee, please. Strong with three sugars."

While I butter my toast, I ask. "Since when has your

husband been missing, Mrs Herriot?" The pupils in the blue eyes dilute and the lip biting continues.

"This morning. Oh no, it must have been in the night. But I found out this morning. He wasn't in his room. Not in any of our rooms."

"Anything missing? Clothes, valise? Left a note where he is?"

She shakes her head making the blonde curls around her face dance.

"Nothing. He just vanished from the face of the earth."

"Did you have an argument preceding his departure?"

"We did." The blue eyes fill with tears that look genuine enough. "But nothing excessive. Nothing that would make... make him leave me for good."

"Leave you for good? Who says Mr Herriot has left you for good? As far as I see it, he may walk into that door any minute and tell you he went to buy a box of cigars."

At that very moment, the door to the breakfast room opens, and I catch my breath. However, I am not quite that good, and instead we see Catherine walk in looking as flustered and red as Winnifred Herriot was moments before.

14

A TRIP TO THE PYRAMIDS

Shepheard's Hotel Breakfast Room still at breakfast, 13 July 1896

"No time to lose, Immy!" Catherine cries out when she arrives at my table, completely ignoring Winnifred, which is quite a rude thing to do, of course. "I'll ask the staff to pack up luncheon for us. I've arranged for transport to take us to Giza today. We should leave now. It's a once-in-a-lifetime opportunity, as there will be a British tour guide, I know leading the excursion. You simply must hear him talk!"

"What's the hurry, Catherine?" I ask rising, with my gaze resting on Mrs Herriot, who stares up at me in dismay.

"Edmund Worthington is worth our hurry," my cousin answers with a I-don't-take-no-for-an-answer look in her green eyes. "Sir Edmund is as experienced and knowledgeable a guide as we can get. I've known him for years. He is ever so passionate about sharing his expertise on the history of the pyramids, and he's utterly charming. You'll love him."

And he may have information about your C, I reply in silence, as I take leave of Mrs Herriot, and my breakfast, without making any promise to find her husband. Even if I wanted to help her, which isn't likely, it would be impossible. How could I, a foreigner in this country, be able to help with finding a British citizen? She must go to the police herself if she's really thinking his absence is something serious.

Before we embark on this erratic excursion that is suddenly etched in my cousin's mind, I try to talk sense to her. But to no avail.

"What's the rush running out before I even finished my breakfast, which was already cooked and is getting cold?"

"It's at least an hour's ride, maybe two, if we encounter setbacks. The camels are slow and there's an absolute need to arrive at the pyramids before the hottest time of the day. Oh Immy, I thought you'd be excited about this but all you do is grumble."

"Camels?" I exclaim in horror. "Do camels draw carts here in Egypt?"

"No silly, we sit on them. They're ever so comfortable and really cute. Just slow and wilful at times, but I told Ahmed to get us the more expensive ones that are usually a little better behaved."

"I'm not going to sit atop a camel. Not in my lifetime." I resolutely cross my arms over my chest. "And I'm not leaving Jasper another day with the staff either. He was sick most of the night on something they fed him that didn't agree with his tender stomach."

"Immy, no! You can't do this to me. I promise you'll have a day like no other in your life. Please, just say yes." Catherine is actually pleading with me in the middle of the Breakfast Room, and I become more exasperated with the situation by the minute. First Winnifred Herriot wanting me to find her husband, Ralph and now Catherine thinking that sitting atop a camel for hours and being dragged around a pyramid site is my most desirable day.

"You go if it means so much to you," I suggest. "I'm perfectly happy staying in the garden reading 'The Portrait of a Lady' by Henry James. I've been wanting to read it for years and specifically brought it with me on this trip."

The idea of sitting in the shade with a tall glass of cooled mint tea and my book and Jasper at my feet presents itself as far more pleasant than riding through the desert atop a camel, the more I think of it the more appealing it becomes.

"But I've seen the Great Pyramid many times, Immy. I'm not doing this for myself, I'm doing this for you!" Catherine looks taken aback and for a moment I believe she'll burst out in tears. Then I remember my silent promise to help her with her love affair.

I sigh and consent to her plan, though with a compromise. "I'll go, but only if you find us a horse-drawn carriage and Jasper can come as well."

"I'll dash out immediately to take care of that and on my way out I'll order your breakfast to be packed up for the ride. How about that?"

"If that's what you want," I give in, "then what can I say?"

Catherine actually kisses both my cheeks and I submit to the fact I'm apparently making her very happy doing this for her. Personally, I care as little as the size of my thumb about the pyramids. I know that's a terrible thing to say, but what is so interesting about giant blocks of sand filled with mummies that possibly smell and hieroglyphs I can't decipher?

Catherine doesn't stop babbling as we're seated in a rickety carriage, the springs of which creek and sigh, and the upholstery of which is quite worn and a bit niffy.

"Do you realize the Great Pyramid of Giza is thousands of years old, Immy? Can you imagine ancient Egyptians building them block after block until they'd created one of the most iconic and mysterious structures in the entire world? Not that they were conscious of that, of course! People knew so little of the world at large, hardly ever travelling beyond their borders. At least, that is what we understand to be true."

I nod, trying to trace the source of Catherine's agitation. Is it just C or is she on another mission as well? Didn't she say something about having to bring artefacts to England? Maybe that Sir Edmund is the go between. Bah, it's all so complicated, and that in this heat!

I need to keep giving Jasper little sips of water from a bowl we're brought with us, but he huffs and puffs like a proper steam engine and I'm afraid his old heart will fail. No thoughts of that.

"Can we go inside the Pyramid? I suppose it will be cool inside?"

Catherine looks at me as if I'm pinheaded.

"Of course, what would be the use if you could only

gawk at it from the outside? The questions you some-times ask, Cousin."

She shakes her head in wonder but I'm content with the answer. I'm not going to stand in that oversized sandpit for longer than absolutely necessary. It's probably smelly and draughty inside but I'm just going to focus my attention on Catherine, so I'll manage. And I have my perfumed hanky with me just in case. As long as Jasper doesn't start yapping at the dead bodies.

It takes a while for the old carriage to leave Cairo, and I'm surprised at the number and variety of transportation going in the same direction as us. People riding on horse-back or utilizing carriages, and indeed the camels Catherine so commended. The animals look enormous and sluggish, and smelly!

To my amazement I see women also sitting on top of the beasts, not just Egyptian women dressed entirely in black, but even tourists, their skirts tucked around them, their heads veiled against the sun, the sand and the wind but looking all smug and modern.

"Not for me," I profess aloud and Catherine giggles.

"You don't know what you're missing, Immy. It's great fun."

"And probably sun stroke in the bargain," I grumble. "No thanks."

Leaving the city we travel westward, passing through an arid and sandy desert that looks to me as if we've landed on the moon. Not very attractive and despite the cover of the carriage, the heat of July is intense, with the sun casting a scorching glare over the horizon.

Finally, the pyramids come into view, their massive

forms rising majestically against the deep blue sky. Against my better judgment, I'm captivated at their sight.

"The Great Pyramid of Giza is also known as the Pyramid of Khufu," Catherine explains. "Though there are three pyramids in a row, this colossus dominates the landscape with its imposing size. It's also remarkably precisely constructed."

"It's ... it's quite something," I admit, struck as I am by the magnitude and grandeur of this Great Pyramid.

"You see!" Catherine says triumphantly. "I knew you would be disappointed if you hadn't come. Do you know it's actually 481 feet tall? I still can't believe it's been the tallest man-made structure in the world for over 3,800 years. The sheer scale of it is unimaginable. Every living creature should see it with their own eyes."

I'm all eyes. It's true. Even Jasper seems to glance out of the window in awe.

The carriage comes to an abrupt halt.

"Inside," Catherine orders.

"I'm glad you convinced me to come," I say. And I mean it.

15

A MOST UNCOMMON DISCOVERY

*Grand Pyramid of Giza, later that same day, 13
July 1896*

"Welcome ladies. What an honour, what an honour." An exceedingly tall and stick-like man with a rather large head adorned with a crop of thick sandy-blond hair, stretches out a bony hand and grips mine quite firmly.

"Mrs Lynch, welcome to Giza. What an honour to finally meet you." He pumps my hand as if he's extracting water from a well, the owl-grey eyes scanning my face as if I'm an old acquaintance.

"Thank you!" I reply, finding the scholar rather peculiar but not unfriendly. Jasper sniffs his trousers as if he's doubtful about the man's credentials as well.

"So, is this really your first time to this extraordinary sanctuary, Mrs Lynch?" Sir Edmund shakes his head in wonder which make his grey side whiskers move rhythmically with his jaw. Catherine hops from one foot to the other, clearly wanting the attention on her now.

"It is," I say with a candid smile, "and it's all due to my dear cousin, Catherine."

"Of course, of course," the scholar replies. "Mrs C is a regular, aren't you, my dear?" And to my surprise, he kisses her as if she is his sister. I'm quite aghast at his liberties but Catherine kisses him back and says teasingly, "Oh Eddy, you're quite something, but it's true. You and I know this Pyramid front to back and vice versa. High time to show it to Immy."

I find the tone between the two quite familial and untoward but when invited to follow them inside the cool of the monument, I follow hastily. Jasper trips along by my side as if we're going on an adventure. Which I guess we probably are.

My eyes take time to adjust to the darkness inside, seeing only the contours of the interior before I can discern what the shapes are meant to be. We meander through narrow passages and dimly lit chambers, adding an air of mystery to the experience. Sir Edmund's voice is a drone of facts and figures that go way above my head, but Catherine hangs on his every word as if she is hearing the story for the first time.

Often, she complements his explanation with all sorts of intelligent titbits he omitted. They are like a well-oiled machine together and it crosses my mind my cousin might have been a tour guide here once herself. Otherwise, why comment she knows the Pyramid front to back?

Either they consider me a disinterested tourist, or they need to catch up so dearly they have forgotten my presence. They're soon deep in discussion with each other and reasoning over what apparently was recently discovered by the famous Egyptologist Flinders Petrie, and not even bothering to keep up the pretence of engaging me in their tour. They even wander away from me at times and the volume of their voices drops to a whisper.

Aha, just what I thought would happen. Well, let her. I hope she gets her answers. I tell myself. I need to watch where I place my feet anyway and have an obligation to make sure Jasper doesn't break a leg either. It's not that I'm not interested in what is at display. The hieroglyphic inscriptions and intricate carvings on the walls are impressive and the mise-en-scene mysterious.

I can understand some people's fascination with the beliefs and actions of ancient cultures. It's just that I'm more interested in the world of today and in living people more than anything in history. I find myself studying how Catherine and Sir Edmund communicate with each other and especially what they don't say but imply, and the hints of conversation about the whereabouts of the mysterious Mr C. Certainly more than going all head-over-heels for the loves and sorrows of our distant ancestors.

As we venture deeper and deeper into the pyramid's belly, we finally reach what Sir Edmund explains is the burial chamber, the final resting place of Pharaoh Khufu. It's a rather large but low-ceilinged space with an enormous sarcophagus in the middle.

"Is the Pharaoh still in there?" I ask, wrinkling my nose.

"Alas, alas," Sir Edmund wails, his voice echoing

against the stone walls, "the pharaoh's remains have long been removed by grave robbers. We don't know exactly when that happened but probably many centuries ago.

What would robbers do with an old mummy? I wonder but don't ask.

Catherine and the guide keep moving around the sarcophagus, pointing at this and that and I'm beginning to grow bored, and thirsty, so I wander around in the anteroom to the burial chamber in search of a place to sit down and wait for them.

Jasper pulls me in the direction of what looks like another, smaller sarcophagus. When I look inside, I'm sure I'm going to faint! With all my willpower I stay upright, grasping the cool stone of the tomb to steady myself.

Surrounded by low, hardened clay walls lies a white mummy, wrapped up in strips of linen. Even the face is hidden. It looks fresh and clean. Wait, clean?! That doesn't fit with all the dusty and mouldy objects we've encountered so far. *Why would an ancient mummy be clean and white after all this time?*

Filing that thought away, I steel myself for another glance. I find myself startled yet again. But it's not so much the mummy that startles me, it's something that glints in the light of my flickering torch. What is it? I inch closer, curious, while I glance around me to see if someone will stop me from going too close to the tomb. Jasper and I are the only ones in the dim-lit space and no uniformed attendant rushes up. I can hear Catherine and Edmund's voices in the room next door.

"Should I inform them, or take a look myself, Roly-Poly?" I wonder aloud as my instinct already draws me nearer and nearer, shortening Jasper's leash so he's close to my side. "You'll just have to come up with me." I expect Jasper to balk, refusing to verge upon a dead body. My dog's total disinterest in what lies in those sheets is a second surprise to me. Not even a twitch of his nostrils.

I listen to the voices next-door once more. They're not coming nearer, so I take a chance and finger the loose linen flap at the mummy's side, lifting it deftly so I can inspect the gleaming thing underneath.

Heavens, it's a pocket watch! I might not know much about ancient Egypt, but even I instantly know this is odd. The new linen and a modern pocket watch. Certainly, that last item doesn't belong in an Egyptian pyramid. I direct the light of my torch to inspect the gold watch up close. And the torch illuminates a faint inscription: *To Our Darling Son, RH. Love Always, Mum & Dad.*

RH? I gasp, don't believe my eyes, blink, and feel sick in my stomach. Who can RH be? My first thought is that these are Ralph Herriot's initials but why on earth? And how?!

"It could be anyone's watch! Someone is playing a prank on someone else," I assure myself in a stage whisper, as I feel Jasper protesting on his leash at being held so tight. I'm still looking at the nicely engraved golden watch, good quality, an E.D. Johnson, the respected London watchmaker and founder of the British Horological Institute.

I am at a loss as to whether or not I should cry out to Catherine and Edmund to come and have a look, but my intuition tells me to keep quiet for some reason. Don't ask me why. The less said about it, the better, it seems. It's too surreal, a prank for certain. If RH is indeed Ralph

Herriot, is it Winnifred behind this? But she didn't know I was going to be here. Who knew?

Or maybe I don't have anything to do with it and have merely stumbled upon it by accident. And why would someone want to pretend Ralph Herriot, an industrialist from Dartmond in rural England, was killed and lain in a burial site inside the Great Pyramid of Gaza? What sort of morbid prank is this?

My mind – already in solve-the-mystery mode – is working overtime until my common sense takes over. This is too outlandish to be true. Though I feel as if committing an act of sacrilege, my intuition is to put Jasper inside the tomb and let him have a good sniff. What happens is just as I expect. He's not terribly interested, sniffs the linen, and looks up at me with eyes that say, "What do you want me to tell you, Mistress?" I have my answer then, as I lift him to the floor again. Whatever there is under that linen, it's not a body. Ralph Herriot is not in there. It's most certainly a prank. But why, and why something so outlandish?

"Imogene where are you?" Catherine's voice gets louder as she approaches the entrance to the antechamber but something in me decides to hide this mummy surrounded in mysteries from her. I don't know why. Protection? Fear? Wanting to solve the puzzle myself?

"Coming!" I call back. Jasper and I quickly exit the chamber and follow Sir Edmund and my cousin outside. My mind is running wild again. Should I tell Winnifred? I decide against it. I'll study her meticulously to see if she betrays herself. Because I'm eighty percent sure RH stands for Ralph Herriot and she is behind this and wants someone to find the mummy and report it to her. Why, I have no idea, but she's definitely up to something. It can be reported by someone *else*, as another drove of tourists enters the pyramid as we leave.

I also study my cousin and her new best friend. Are they in on this as well? But why would they? As far as I know Catherine doesn't even know of the Herriots' existence, though it may be a sign to the contrary that she completely ignored Winnifred at the breakfast table.

But if my two guides had been interested whether I found a peculiar mummy or not they would have shown more interest in my reaction, and at least made sure to be in the room when I found it. No, the chief culprit of this so-called disappearance is Mrs Ralph Herriot herself. Only, why would she go to such lengths of setting up this elaborate scene? Well, my job is laid out for me. If I find the answer to that question, I think the truth will unravel like a mummy unwrapped.

MORE QUESTIONS THAN ANSWERS

The Shepheard's Hotel, later that same day, 13 July 1896

"Do you mind if I lie down for an hour or so? I think the heat is getting to me?" I ask Catherine as we descend from the carriage in front of Shepheard's Hotel.

"Not at all, Immy. I just hope Eddy and I weren't neglecting you at the Pyramids. I hadn't realized how much I'd missed him. He's a dear, dear friend."

"Oh no," I reply. "I'm glad you were able to catch up with a friend and I've seen quite enough sarcophaguses for a while. Will Sir Edmund be going back to England soon?"

I don't miss seeing Catherine's face cloud over. "Yes, Eddy's due to return to England at the end of this week. He's been here for a couple of months, but the British Museum wants him back."

I can't help myself. She looks so stricken. "And did he

have any news on your other friend, the one you refer to as C?"

Now guilt creeps over my cousin's face and with a deep sigh, she replies, "Eddy did, in fact. He confirmed that C is in Egypt, but Eddy hasn't been able to get hold of him. I'm afraid, Immy, that something has happened to him."

"But why?" I ask, while we enter the hotel's foyer and make our way up to our rooms.

"It's not like C to ignore Eddy nor me."

"But how do you know then that he is still in Egypt?"

"Because the British Museum sent him, that's why. C's here to replace Sir Edmund."

"I see. Well, I hope he shows up in good health soon and your worries were for nought," I say as I open the door to my rooms and let Jasper slip in. "Shall we meet up for dinner, then?"

Catherine nods.

SLEEP IS FAR from my mind as I sit down in my chair and my gaze wanders over the boats slowly gliding down the Nile River. I know what I need to do but it seems outlandish and a risk. And yet it feels like the only way forward. I must write Winnifred Herriot a note to confront her about her mummy trick. What if someone steals that expensive watch? I tucked it deeper into the folds of linen, but a sharp eye would likely detect it. And who knows how quickly the fresh linen would be noticed in contrast to the ancient state of the draping in other tombs.

But how do I word it? I don't know the woman and maybe I shouldn't get involved in the first place. It's tricky waters.

And what if Ralph Herriot is playing along with his wife for some reason? Maybe they have money problems in England, and he is trying to act as if he's dead, so they won't have to pay? I think all I can do is confront her at this stage and then let it rest.

I grab my notepad and pen when there's a knock on my door. Thinking it will be one of the staff, I open the door only to almost get it banged into my face.

"He's dead! My darling Ralph is dead! His body has been found inside the pyramids!" A hysterical Winnifred cries as she rushes into my room like a storm.

Sobbing and tearing at her hair, she falls into one of my chairs. I'm too flabbergasted to react, either to her rudeness bursting into my room unannounced like this, or to her grief which seems genuine enough. Instead, I shut the door to find myself confronted by a woman who's beside herself in every possible way.

Not knowing how to approach her, slightly worried she might attack me with those long nails of her, I keep standing near the door, so I can be assured of a quick exist into the corridor to seek help should I need to.

"Now, now," I call over her lamentations. "Please calm yourself, Mrs Herriot, it's not as bad as you think it is." But she doesn't seem to hear me, and as suddenly as she came in, she runs towards me. The anger in her eyes is severe.

"Let me out!" she cries. "You're useless, useless!"

"Alright," I reply calmly. "If that's what you want. Just

know that while it might be Ralph Herriot's watch lying in that sarcophagus, it's certainly not his body."

"What are you talking about, you silly cat?! I don't need you!" she shouts, rushing along the corridor and down the stairs. I shake my head angrily, offended at being called a silly cat.

"Just as well," I say aloud, as I go inside again. "Just as well. I'm glad to no longer be involved in your shoddy affairs," I say to the empty room.

"Immy, what's all that shouting?" Catherine, her eyes sleepy and confused, stands in the connecting doors between our apartments.

"Nothing, Catherine. Just a hysterical hotel guest who mistook me for someone else."

"But was she in your room? Are you alright? Did she hurt you in any way?"

"Yes, I'm alright. I'm sure the staff will handle her."

"But why was she here? Did you know her? Who was she?"

"Ah Catherine, let's forget it and go and have dinner downstairs. It's been a long day."

Catherine eyes me suspiciously but seeing I'm adamant to let the matter rest, she doesn't try again.

But my peace is short-lived. Catherine and I are just about to start on our chicken soup when two imposing Egyptian men in uniform march into the dining room. Jasper snarls and I hush him. I look up at the men in dismay when they stop at our table. What's going on now?

"Are you Mrs Lynch?"

"I am. And who are you?" I'm not impressed by

uniforms. I've lived with uniformed men all my life. From my father the general to my husband the constable.

"The hotel manager tells me you are possibly the last person who saw Mrs Winnifred Herriot before she went missing."

"She went what?!" I gasp but then I see Catherine across the table from me turn white like a ghost.

"Mrs Wini... Winnifred Herriot?" She stutters, her eyes wide, "what is *she* doing here?"

"You know her?" I look at my cousin in utter bewilderment.

"Never mind," one of the police officers intervenes. "Could you come with us for a moment, Mrs Lynch? It will just be a minute. A short statement is all we need."

17

MRS HERRIOT GOES MISSING
AS WELL

Shepheard's Hotel, later that evening, 13 July 1896

With one more look at Catherine, who's taken to staring out of the window, I follow the policemen to the lobby.

"Apologies for interrupting your dinner," the elder of the police-officers, a man with an imposing black moustache and flabby dark cheeks, eyes like dark pools, says.

Mr Zech has discretely manoeuvred us into an empty room where we can talk without being seen or overheard. A waiter brings in tall glasses of lemonade and hurries out as if he's seen a bad omen.

"It's no problem," I say in a friendly tone. "I was married for thirty years to a police officer, so I know everything about interrupted meals." This makes the black moustached man smile, while the younger one takes a notepad and pen from his coat pocket.

"We'll keep it brief," he promises, "and you'll probably know the kind of questions we'll ask."

"I'm just curious…" I react, "who reported Mrs Herriot as missing?"

"Her husband did, Mr Herriot. He seemed quite unperturbed. But we Egyptians find it hard to read the English. You are so much more close-lipped and unemotional than we are."

I digest this information with interest. So, Ralph is the culprit, pretending to be missing only to report his wife missing instead. Strange games these two are playing. I push to the back of my mind Catherine's reaction to Winnifred's missing. I'll deal with that later.

"Was there no body found at the pyramids today? That of Mr Herriot wrapped up as a mummy? And an expensive pocket watch by his side?"

The police officer looks at me in surprise.

"Not that I know of, Mrs Lynch. But we'll have it checked."

"Don't bother," I say, "it wasn't real anyway."

He now looks at me as if I'm soft in the head, but the younger man writes everything down.

"So, please tell us when you last saw Mrs Herriot and under what circumstances."

I tell them all that happened from the breakfast meeting to her stormy interruption in my room in the afternoon. I keep it light-hearted, as I'm sure it's only some staged scenario and nothing serious.

With that, the policemen and I part ways again. I promise them I'll keep an eye out for any news I hear about Mrs Herriot. Then I rejoin Catherine in the dining room.

I'm done with everyone playing games around me, so I immediately confront her.

"How do you know Mrs Herriot?"

But Catherine has become all evasive. "I don't know her personally. I know of her."

"From Dartmond?"

"Yes."

Catherine plays with her fork, drawing trails through the gravy on her empty plate, not looking me in the eye. I feel my curiosity rise. And a vague sense of dismay. Something's going on here, but I can't put my finger on it. As long as Catherine has nothing to do with this whole charade with the missing Herriots. Because I'm quite convinced it's the spouses playing pranks on each other, For whatever bizarre reason.

I told the policemen that as well. Not to put their whole force on a couple that's playing hide and seek in some obnoxious, publicly dramatized way.

"Then why did you look so shocked when you heard she went missing?"

"I didn't know she was here in Cairo. Honestly, Immy, that's all. I may have overreacted."

"You seemed upset, yes."

"I'm alright now. So why did the policemen talk with you? Was that about the yelling in your room this afternoon?" Catherine's shoulders are hunched. She seems miserable and I feel sorry for her but don't know how to help her.

"Yes. That was Mrs Herriot. This morning she informed me her husband went missing."

"What?" Now Catherine does look up. She looks terrified.

"You mean you know Ralph Herriot as well?" I ask, thinking Catherine is overreacting again.

"What?" she barely whispers. "Ralph? Yes Ralph, of course. Is he missing as well?"

"Catherine, for Heaven's sake, what is the matter? Can't you trust me? Are they friends of yours? Anyway, don't worry about them. They are just being silly. I'm sure of it. Neither of them is really missing."

"What do you mean *neither of them is really missing?*" Catherine asks bewildered. "How can you know that, Immy? Did they tell you?"

"No!" I say resolutely. "But to be honest I'm quite done with the topic. Everybody is acting strangely. If you don't mind, I don't want to talk about it anymore. Can we not just enjoy being here in Egypt and forget about silly English people causing fake drama abroad?"

Catherine looks sheepish. "Alright, if that's what you want, Immy."

"Yes, that's what I want. Let's have dessert. I'm craving a slice of Victoria sponge cake. And now you can call me odd, as I never crave food otherwise."

And I can't wait to get to my room to think things through. But I don't tell Catherine that.

18

A TRIP TO THE POST OFFICE

Cairo Post Office, the next day, 14 July 1896

I fall into a fitful sleep, as my mind hasn't solved any part of the puzzle. And I don't like that. I want to understand. I want pieces to fit. But nothing fits. Not Catherine's odd behaviour from the beginning of our trip. Not the Herriots going missing, or presumably going missing, from the Shepheard's Hotel. Not the pretend mummy with the E.D. Johnson pocket watch in the sarcophagus inside the pyramid. Not my involvement with it all.

"Oh Thaddeus," I say in the night, tossing and turning, "what am I missing here? What am I not seeing?"

And, as with a flash of lightning, I get an idea that I will act on in the morning. Now I can sleep. Jasper lying next to me on the bed (yes, I have indulged him this entire holiday) and at least one coherent thought in my head.

"Thank you, my benedict," I whisper as I fall asleep.

The next morning I'm up early and take my breakfast before everyone else. Then I ask directions to the nearest post office. As it's only down the street from the hotel, I decide to walk and take Jasper for an early stroll with me.

Though it promises to become another swelteringly hot day, I'm quite comfortable under my parasol at the moment, and enjoy the walk along the Nile River with a view of the boats and the softly lapping waves on the shoreline.

When I arrive at the post office it's already a bustling hub of activity, despite the early hour. The place is obviously an essential part of the city's communication network. Located on a busy crossroad, the building is a mix of traditional Egyptian architecture and influences from the European colonial period. The stone building features a grand facade with intricate designs, arched windows, and ornate detailing.

Upon entering the post office, Jasper and I are greeted by a spacious and high-ceilinged lobby, sporting chandeliers, elaborate mouldings, and murals depicting historical scenes and landscapes. But I have no time and little eye for sightseeing right now.

I head towards the main counter, where I see other customers conducting their postal business, hoping the clerks dressed in formal uniforms will understand English. Behind them are numerous shelves for postal supplies, including stamps, envelopes, and writing materials.

Which section would send international telegrams? There is no way I can decipher the sections labelled in Arabic. I look around me, slightly bewildered. One section has rows of wooden post office boxes, where people are busy bringing and receiving their correspondence. In another area, employees are diligently sorting incoming and outgoing mail - letters and packages in all sizes and formats.

I walk over to another section that I hope offers telegraph services. It looks as if the employees here are telegraph operators, stationed in a separate room, busily tapping out messages on telegraph keys and relaying them to their intended destinations.

"Hello?" I ask when I see no bell to announce my arrival at this counter.

I try again over the sounds of people conversing, the rustle of paper, and the occasional ringing of telegraph machines. The air is tinged with the scent of ink and the faint aroma of envelopes and packages.

"Hello, Sir?"

A balding operator with thick glasses on the bridge of his nose, looks up and in my direction. He waves one hand in the air while continuing to type with the fingers of his other hand. As if saying, *Patience, Ma'am. We're all in a hurry here.* Nothing happens so I wonder if I should draw attention to myself again. Jasper has collapsed at my feet his snout on my shoe.

Then finally the balding man rises and comes towards the counter. He limps considerably and looks peevish.

"Yes, Ma'am?" He must have seen I was English and addresses me in my own tongue.

"I'd like to send a telegram to Dartmond in the Cotswolds in England," I say, clearly pronouncing every word, wondering if I should spell it on paper for him. But he answers in fluent English.

"Very well, Ma'am. Contents of your telegram, please?"

Now I falter. How to exactly word the message to Mr Banerjee, Mayor of Dartmond? The clerk takes me in with dark-brown eyes, notepad and pen ready. In a friendly voice, he says, suddenly sounding as if he has all the time in the world. "Take your time, Ma'am. These messages need careful consideration of each word."

I give him a grateful glance. "Let's make it..." I begin. "In Cairo. Mr and Mrs R Herriot missing. Any information from Dartmond? Mrs I Lynch."

The balding clerk writes while I speak the words and then pushes his notepad under my nose.

"Like this?"

He's written it down almost perfectly. I only need to correct the name Herriot which he's written with single 'r' and Dartmond has become Darkmond.

"Thank you," I say. "When can you send it, Sir?"

"Not so fast, Ma'am." He scribbles some more on his pad, then reads,

"In Cairo. Stop. Mr and Mrs R Herriot missing. Stop. Any information from Dartmond? Stop. Mrs I Lynch. Stop."

"Yes," I reply. "That's correct."

"Every word matters," he repeats.

"It does," I agree.

"I will send it straightaway, Ma'am. I take it that you are lodging at the Shepheard's Hotel? As soon as there is a reply, I will send one of the junior clerks with it."

"Thank you," I say gratefully, taking my purse from my handbag. But the balding man with the glasses keeps scanning me over.

"You do not look at all like a detective, Ma'am, if you don't mind me saying so."

Now it's my turn to stare at him.

"Heaven's, I'm not a detective, Sir. My husband was a constable, but I'm not involved in any of that."

"Ah, but you are, Mrs Lynch," he observes with conviction. I nod. What else could I do?

And with this observation, I step back into the hot Cairo sun.

"You are," the trees along the riverbank seem to whisper and I look up at the sky. "Oh Thaddeus," I mumble. "Is it true? Is this what you want for me?"

The trees sigh and wave their tops in the gentle breeze. Jasper wags his tail.

"I am," I agree reluctantly.

19

ANOTHER MOST UNCOMMON DISCOVERY

Shepheard's Hotel, later that same day, 14 July 1896

On my way back from the post office, I decide to not put any more pressure on my poor cousin. It doesn't seem to work. Catherine's life must have been one of hiding truths from everyone due to her estranged marriage and her affair with C. If I push too hard, I may only estrange her from me as well.

I know that Mr Banerjee will not just take my telegram at face value. He's the kind of man who will dive into the matter, read the papers to scan for messages of missing English tourists in Egypt, circumspectly inquire with people who may know the Herriots better. Only then will he reply with the facts he has gathered.

I also like the idea that someone back home knows I'm involved in another 'mystery case'. Just in case. This is, after all, a foreign and perhaps dangerous country where locals may think British people wear many riches on them. Or if there *is*, after all, some kind of conspiracy behind the Herriots' disappearance that I'm not picking up on, it might drag me into a sordid mess against my will. I'm in it up to my ears anyway.

Catherine is out when I return to the hotel, which gives me time to sort the affairs in my head. I decide to tap on Mr Zech's office door.

"I beg your pardon, Sir, but is there any news of the missing couple?"

He looks up from the ledger he was writing in, and I see he's much perturbed.

"Bad case altogether, Mrs Lynch, bad case," he repeats in his strong German accent. "Puts the hotel in a bad light for the folks back in Europe."

"But do you know whether they disappeared from their rooms here or somewhere in Cairo?"

"No, Mrs Lynch, I know as little as you do. You spoke with the Egyptian police last night, didn't you?"

"Yes, I did. And I came in to see if there was any more news on the case, but I understand there isn't."

I see no reason to inform the hotelier of my trip to the post office. I've long learned not to tell people things before there is proof in the pudding. It just takes their minds in directions they oughtn't go into.

"I'll go upstairs then, Mr Zech. My apologies for the interruption."

"No apologies needed, Mrs Lynch. I'm actually thankful that a lady with such a clear mind occupies herself with these sordid affairs. I understand your husband was a very respected head constable in the Cotswolds."

"He was, Mr Zech, bless his soul. And thank you for the compliment."

∼

I DON'T HAVE to wait long for a reply from Mr Banerjee. Some hours later, a junior staff member from the post office delivers the British telegram that I turn in my hands for a while before opening it. Stalling as if it entails a message I don't want to read. But then I scold myself for my chicken-heartedness.

"Mr Lynch never shied from a task, did he, Jasper? So, neither should I." For some reason I feel reassured talking to my sleeping dog while I pick up the letter opener and tear open the flimsy blue paper.

> Mr R Herriot in Dartmond as usual.
> Stop. Dr C Herriot reported missing in Egypt.
> Stop. No mention of Mrs Herriot. Stop.
> Yours, Mayor B. Stop.

I CAN'T SUPPRESS a cry of surprise. The shorthand of the telegraph has just presented something that never occurred to me. Is it just a coincidence or could C Herriot be Catherine's mysterious C? That would explain she was shocked to find out the Herriots' were here. The same last name.... a brother, a cousin?

But still, it all makes little to no sense. If Ralph Herriot is in Dartmond then how can he have been at the breakfast table with his wife only two days earlier, when I know just how long and arduous the journey from England to Cairo is?

Why are my brain cells operating so slowly? Slow or not, while I'm sipping my afternoon tea, the picture is slowly going from blurred to clearer in my mind's eye. Is the picture forming for you too, my Roly-Poly?

Jasper yaps in his sleep, ignoring my relief at beginning to understand the pieces of the puzzle before me.

But a new worry strikes me next. The Dartmond Herriots may enjoy playing practical jokes on each other. Dr C Herriot missing is serious business. Business I must keep from Catherine at all costs, just in case that is her beloved C. Unless her friend, Sir Edmund, has already informed her.

Before I have time to check on Catherine, there is another knock on my door. The policeman with the black moustache and the flabby cheeks stands in the doorway.

"My apologies for disrupting your afternoon, Mrs Lynch, but I have good news and bad," he says, looking quite conspiratorial.

"Do come in, officer. I have new information as well," I reply, inviting him in by opening the door wider. All seems silent in Catherine's quarters. I wonder if she's in or out.

"Ladies first," he insists, as the heavy-set policeman is seated in one of the hotel's ornate armchairs, mopping beads of sweat from his broad forehead with a checked handkerchief.

"There are two Mr Herriots," I explain, "one is safely home in England, Mr Ralph Herriot, and one, Dr C Herriot, is missing in Egypt."

The policeman looks surprised. "I came to inform

you of the missing of Dr *Cornelius* Herriot but apparently, you've already found out by yourself. Clever work indeed! I don't know about a Mr Ralph Herriot apart from you telling me about the artificial mummy at Giza with the golden watch on it."

"Do you have information whether Dr Herriot is related to Mr Ralph Herriot, officer?" I ask.

"Not yet, because our interests haven't been on finding the Ralph Herriot you talked about. We were concerned with Mrs Herriot's missing and now that of her husband."

"Her husband? Surely you are mistaken. Mrs Winnifred Herriot is married to *Mr Ralph* Herriot."

The police officer looks at me as if I'm daft.

"That is not the information I have, Ma'am. And not what Mr Zech has told me. Mrs Winnifred Herriot, who by the way is safely back at the hotel, is married to one Dr Cornelius Herriot."

I'm silent for a minute. My mind making cartwheels until I exclaim. "That explains everything. Well not everything, but a lot!"

"Pray tell me, Ma'am, as I find this all quite a tiresome rigmarole." The heavy policeman mops some more sweat while I tap my fingers together.

20

CALMING CATHERINE

Shepheard's Hotel, that same day, 14 July 1896

There is no time to explain more to the black-moustached policeman as Catherine comes storming into my room, her eyes full of tears and her clothes full of mud.

"He's captured. He's captured!" she cries out. Seeing the police officer sitting in my boudoir cries to him, "Officer, please do something! Do something before he's killed!"

I rise to catch my sobbing cousin in my arms. It's quite a display she makes before a stranger, a man of the law as it is, but I forgive her. My main concern is to calm her down.

"I promise you we'll do all we can to find Dr Herriot," the surprised policeman says, also rising from his chair. "I understand he is a good friend of yours, Mrs Northwind?"

Catherine looks at the man as if he's partly heaven-sent and partly the devil's advocate.

Oh no, I think. *How is she going to explain her relationship to the policeman? And she seems to forget I don't even know C's surname is Herriot.*

But the police officer seems unperturbed by this information.

"We're taking Dr Herriot's disappearance very seriously, Mrs Northwind. Very, very seriously. We know the risk he could be in, but I can share with you we have an idea who is behind it. And it may be more innocent than you think."

The policeman looks at me as if he expects me to agree with him. Which I do, so I nod, as he continues.

"As soon as we know more, I'll come and inform you myself. The name is Inspector Hassan Hamdi Pasha. If there's anything you need, the police station is right down the street and just ask for me. Or inform Mr Zech that you need me, and I'll come as quickly as I can. I bid you good day for now, ladies, and please don't upset yourselves too much. The heat and such worries are not a good combination, I'm afraid." He dabs his forehead for the last time looking worried himself and thus rather contradictory. Then he's out of the door.

I'm still holding Catherine who has stopped sobbing but is trembling like the stem of a reed.

"Do sit down, Cathy, and I'll order us tea," I plead with her, but she keeps hanging onto me.

"I need a drink, a stiff one, not tea!" she cries passionately.

"Alright, I'll ring the bell for a sherry for you and tea for me," I say, leading her to the armchair Inspector Hamdi Pasha just sat in, "but do be calm, please."

"How can I be calm, Immy?" The green eyes are wide

with fear. "You do not know that bandits have wanted to kidnap C for ages. And now it's happened. He knows too much, you see. If he doesn't give them what they want, they'll kill him. Without scruples."

Before I can dive with her into this delicate and complicated matter, I stubbornly wait for tea, letting her babble for the time being. When we're finally seated – Catherine insisted on having a large glass of Courvoisier – and I with my Darjeeling tea with extra sugar, I confront her.

"Is C, Cornelius Herriot, Ralph's twin brother? Are they *identical* twins?"

Catherine looks at me in astonishment. "How did you find that out?"

I shrug. "I have eyes. I've seen Ralph Herriot in Dartmond. I've seen someone who looks like Ralph with Winnifred here in Cairo. But Ralph is in Dartmond, hence the man I saw having breakfast with Winnifred must have been Ralph's identical twin. I'm just angry with myself I didn't see it right from the beginning. I registered something different about him but not enough to see through the charade."

Catherine now gapes at me. Then shakes her head. "Immy, honestly, I knew you were sharp, but I never knew you were *this* sharp. It almost makes me forget my agony. So, you saw C? Here at the hotel, with Winnifred? Why didn't you tell me?"

"Because I just told you, I thought it was Ralph! Why didn't you tell me C was married to Winnifred?"

"How was I to know you knew her? How was I to know she was even here in Egypt? She's never before escorted C here," Catherine says with exasperation in her voice. Then takes a large sip from her glass.

"I don't think there's reason for agony, Cathy." I say softly, "you told me Winnifred and Cornelius had a bad marriage. Winnifred obviously prefers the brother since she lives with him in Dartmond and that is how I know her! Nobody there knows Ralph is not her legal husband."

"What are you implying, Immy? Heavens, you're so wise!"

"I think Winnifred is behind this disappearance..." but then I stop. It makes no sense. The mummy with Ralph's pocket watch on it. Then Winnifred disappearing herself. And now Cornelius. I'm at a loss. But Catherine wants to be comforted.

"What are you saying, Immy? Please finish your sentence."

I hesitate. I don't want to tell my cousin lies but I don't want her to panic either. "It might be a prank Winnifred is playing on her husband. Just to be able to go back to Ralph."

I see Catherine is trying to grasp this, to believe it. And she buys it. "So, he's not kidnapped by bandits? Is that what you're saying?"

"Probably not," I lie, "but we'll have to wait and find out, right?"

21

INTERROGATING WINNIFRED HERRIOT

Shepheard's Hotel, two days later, 16 July 1896

My whole hope of a relaxing vacation in Egypt has gone by the wayside. All I seem to do is run around Cairo trying to find some missing Brits who appear to not be missing, or are only fake-missing, and making sure my cousin doesn't go insane.

And yet I'm having the time of my life! There's nothing like working my brain to get a grip on these seemingly unsolvable situations. So, Jasper and I trudge from the police office to the post office to Mr Zech's office, and back again. In between, I sleep and eat and think.

For a couple of days, I've been trying to get hold of Winnifred Herriot, as I'd like to pose some questions to her, but either she's barricaded herself in her rooms or she's slipped out the backdoor and is already on her way to Ralph in Dartmond. I'm fairly certain it is the latter.

Mr Zech informs me the opposite. According to him,

she is indisposed and in her room. She even refused to speak to Inspector Hamdi Pasha and only lets in one maid, who doesn't speak English, to clean her room and bring her food.

The maid, whom I've tried to interrogate, keeps pointing to her head. I don't know if that means that Mrs Herriot has headaches or that she's not well in the head or its her way of saying she doesn't understand me.

But I'm patient. My Thaddeus has taught me to be patient in these cases. Catherine and I had planned to stay in Egypt for at least two months, so I have another couple of weeks to solve this mystery.

Meanwhile, I do worry about the disappearance of Cornelius Herriot. No sign from him is not a good sign. Catherine is besides herself and practically camps outside Inspector Hamdi Pasha's office on a daily basis. I try to distract her, but she's not interested in excursions or outings. She's even lost her appetite and is a tad too dependent on the Courvoisier, if you ask me.

"You don't understand, Immy. C knows things," she keeps repeating to me as if we all don't *know things*. I do realize that Dr Cornelius Herriot is clearly into something that other people want him out of or has knowledge they want from him, but I'm still sticking with the theory that his estranged wife wanted him out of the way. Now, it is true, whether you die at the hand of a bungling bandit or a waspish wife, it doesn't make much difference.

However, I still believe Winnifred doesn't really mean to kill her husband. She wants something else out of him, be it money or a divorce. But it might have gone out of hand. That's why I need to talk with her. But one nagging thought keeps pestering me about the great resemblance between the Herriot brothers.

As far as I know, nobody in Dartmond doubted for one moment that Ralph wasn't Winnifred's spouse. She could have walked on the arm of either man and people would have believed it was one and the same. So, the chance to finally be free of the real husband, might just have given her motive to do drastic things far away from home. Hadn't Catherine mentioned Winnifred had never before escorted Cornelius to Egypt? Suspicious, indeed.

Oh, I need to talk with her! Urgently. Even Inspector Hamdi Pasha may not get this out of her though I keep him informed of my every step. Well almost every step. As my Benedict used to say to me, *trust yourself first and foremost, my dear, and your second man for 90 %.*

"We could trust each other 100%, dear Thaddeus," I tell the unyielding walls of my hotel room. "That's why we were such a magnificent team when it came to crime solving."

A boat horn hoots from the river. Toot-toot. *Yes dear*, Thaddeus seems to say.

I try one more time. With a box of mint chocolates wrapped up in a cute box, I wrap my knuckles on Room number 12, where Mr Zech told me Winnifred is staying. It's on the second floor not far from my own. The soles of my shoes have trodden this carpeted landing many times in the past days. This time I'm lucky.

The petite and flustered maid who looks after Mrs Herriot's wellbeing opens the door ajar.

"Na'am?" she whispers, which I know means 'yes' in Arabic.

"Mrs Herriot?" I ask.

"Na'am," the small woman nods again.

"Who's that, Layla? If it's that foul-smelling Inspector Pasha, say no."

I have no idea how much English the maid understands but she calls back to the voice inside.

"Lady at door."

"Who is it?"

"It's me, Mrs Lynch." This time Winnifred Herriot is not going to slip through my fingers.

Seconds later, I sit in an armchair identical to the one in my own room, sipping strong Egyptian tea with the proper amount of sugar. Winnifred Herriot, normally as cute and pretty as a September peach, looks waxy around the nose and her eyes have no shine. She pulls on a silk handkerchief between her thin fingers as if she wants to pull out each individual thread. A very different woman from the one who stormed into the breakfast room like a Fury, ordering me to find her husband. A husband I now know she doesn't even want to be married to.

"How are you doing, Mrs Herriot?"

The eyelashes over the porcelain blue eyes flutter and the tearing of the dainty fabric continues.

"What do you expect?" Her voice is husky and low.

"I have no idea," I answer honestly. "I heard you were missing yourself. Can you tell me what happened?"

Some of the fury is back when she yammers, "I was held in a dark room. Can you imagine? And it smelled frightfully. Onions and fried fish. It was beyond horrible." She shudders, then pushes the blond cork curls from her forehead and dabs the silk handkerchief to her temples.

"Could you see anything in that room, even if it was dark? Hear people talk? What language?"

"Heavens!" She looks at me in astonishment. "What kind of questions are those? You sound like an inspector."

"Sorry!" Under my breath I mutter, "and yet you came to me in the beginning."

Then she relaxes a little.

"I forgot you were married to a constable for decades, Mrs Lynch. And you did solve that old case with Miss Platt in Dartmond last year."

Now she manages to surprise me. I'd never thought Winnifred Herriot even looked further than her own nose.

"Yes, that's true, and I assume why you asked for my help earlier, and why I want to help you if I can. I know nothing of Egyptian laws, but I do know a thing or two about solving mysteries."

The whiteness returns to the pretty snub nose.

"I have nothing to do with Cornelius's disappearance if that's what you're trying to say."

"Ho ho ho," I stop her. "We were discussing *your* kidnapping. We'll come to that of your husband's in a minute. The two *may* be related, after all."

The blue eyes look a tad too innocent and the fact she reacted so fast about not having anything to do with her husband's disappearance, coupled with showing no interest in the danger he might be in, tells me volumes.

"I understand you don't want to go back to your fearful hours of captivity, but if we want to catch those culprits you need to tell me everything. How they caught you, how long the trip was to where they took you, that dark room, all you saw and heard, why they let you go unharmed after a day."

"It was four hours."

My mouth opens and closes like a fish on land. Her ordeal was only four hours. She will certainly forget all about it soon.

"So, what happened?" I ask again.

"I was on my way to the post office," the blue eyes blink. "I wanted to send ...uh...Mr Ralph Herriot a telegram." The blue eyes blink faster. "Then a carriage stopped next to me. Quite a handsome carriage, with two beautiful horses, so I didn't think much of it at first.

The driver called to me and asked in broken English if I needed a lift because it was so hot. A lady, I thought she was English, waved from inside the carriage and I thought, why not? So, I got in. But then the lady stepped out on the other side and the driver went in another direction altogether. He went so fast, I had to hold onto the door handle, and I was beyond scared. It totally spooked me. That was all."

She ends abruptly. The story is as illogical as a black-smith in a white silk apron, but I feign interest.

"What happened then?"

"I cried to him to stop. To let me out! I banged on the windows to attract attention from the people in the streets. We went quite far out of Cairo, but I could still see the river. It was late afternoon, you know, still light outside."

"And then?"

"The driver suddenly stopped in front of a house that looked normal. He grabbed me by the arm and took me inside. I was put in a room, and he closed the door. The shutters were closed from the outside but through the cracks I could see some light. The room had a chair and table, a carpet on the floor. I heard voices in the house. They spoke Arabic. I tried the door, but it was locked."

"Did you call for help?"

"Of course!" The blue eyes are fiery again, "I called until I was coarse. I still am." She coughed once and pulled on the handkerchief again.

"An Egyptian woman came in. She brought me tea and sweet things on a tray. I tried to make a dash for the door but the man, that driver, stood there and blocked my way."

"Did they ask you questions? Did they want something? Money? Jewellery?"

Winnifred shakes her head, irritated.

"There was one strange thing, though," she says pensively. "They didn't speak much English, but the man kept asking me. Ralph? Mummy? You see?"

"Aha," I say. "Were you supposed to go to the Great Pyramid of Giza last week?"

"Yes, Cornelius had planned for me to go but I was unwell."

I nod. Things are starting to make sense to me, though I still don't know who did what. I'm not going to tell her everything, though. What she doesn't already know, she needn't know. What I need is to put a finger on Mrs Winfred Herriot's motives, and I think I'm coming closer to the truth.

22

DR AMELIA FAIRCHILD ENTERS THE SCENE

Egyptian Museum, Cairo, the same day, 16 July 1896

Suddenly I'm in a terrible hurry. I get up from my chair and bid Mrs Herriot farewell.

"Don't you want to hear the rest of my absolutely dreadful ordeal?" she squeaks.

"Some other day, Mrs Herriot. I'm glad you're safe and well now, but I remember I have an important errand."

And I dash out of her hotel room, whisk into my own, wake Jasper and with the sleepy Roly-Poly on my heels make my way to Inspector Hassan Hamdi Pasha's office.

The game is over, I think to myself. *Now we get to the serious stuff.* I have no hard proof, but this is what I think:

Cornelius played a prank on his wife about her lover – his own twin-brother! - now that she was alone with her legal husband in Egypt. Not a deadly prank, just something to scare her a little. Winnifred was supposed to see the fake mummy in the tomb to make her worry, but she never got to the pyramids.

Whether Cornelius wants his wife back by pretending her lover is dead or this is his way of saying goodbye to her or just a cruel punishment for adultery, I haven't figured out yet. However, *I* saw the mummy instead of Winnifred, and then Jasper immediately broke the spell by making it clear there was no body inside that pile of fresh linen.

Maybe that was the whole idea. Cornelius is an Egyptologist. He knows no freshly embalmed mummy ends up in an age-old pyramid. But that prank fell flat when Winnifred never saw it. Then he arranged for Winnifred's short but far-from-dangerous kidnap. Why he would organize these events for his estranged wife and her lover, I don't know. Not yet.

What I also haven't worked out is if Winnifred is involved in Cornelius' disappearance or that it is an independent gang, but I know he is in danger. She may have wanted him out of the way, convenient and far from home. I need the inspector to keep an eye on Mrs Herriot. With Cornelius gone and Ralph in Dartmond, she may take a runner. Inspector Pasha needs to step in and do some proper interrogating. Did she or didn't she hire someone to make her husband disappear?

Before I have time to enter the inspector's office, an out-of-breath clerk in a post office uniform hurries my way.

"Telegram for you, Mrs Lynch." He waves the blue paper in his hand.

"Thank you," I say as I look around for a place where I can sit down to read the, no doubt, unpleasant message. I mean really, when does a telegraph ever relay pleasant information? *One sits down before opening a telegram.* My dear, late mother taught me that. And I've never strayed from that advice.

"Do come into the shade of the post office, Ma'am," the young clerk suggests, and I follow him up the steps and accept a bench in the cool hallway. He even hastens into his office to collect a letter opener for me. I take a deep breath. First, I scan the signer. Mayor Banerjee.

Dr C Herriot disappearance confirmed by British Museum. Stop. Contact Dr Amelia Fairchild. Stop. Egyptian Museum. Good luck. Mayor B. Stop.

"THANK YOU, MR BANERJEE," I say to the flimsy paper in my hand. The mayor confirms what I already thought and though I have no idea who Dr Amelia Fairchild is, I immediately direct my feet to the Egyptian museum in hopes of meeting the fair lady.

The police inspector will have to wait for now. Winnifred Herriot may be cunning, but she can wait as I ascertain what this new Dr Fairchild has to do with Cornelius' disappearance. And I really doubt Winnifred is going to take off, based on the state of her in her hotel room.

I find myself temporarily forgetting my mission, as I stand before the Egyptian Museum, that magnificent institution that holds the key to unlocking the ancient mysteries of the pharaohs. Though I've recently professed mummies and sarcophaguses don't hold my interest, now I'm here where scholars study all those secrets, I am in awe as I'm always in awe of people who take their profession seriously. Oh, Catherine, you are just as passionate even without the formal profession.

No wonder my thoughts wander to Catherine. She must have climbed these stairs so often, to enter this treasure trove of artefacts from the rich and awe-inspiring history of the Nile civilization.

As I step through the grand entrance, a sense of anticipation and wonder washes over me. A gold-edged plaque proudly states the museum was recently established by the efforts of dedicated Egyptologists and archaeologists, both from Egypt and from other countries, among which Great Britain is the obvious leader. Inside, the air is thick with the scent of history, the echo of footsteps, and the murmurs of excited visitors.

The museum itself is an architectural marvel. As with all the important buildings in Cairo, it blends elements of traditional Egyptian design with a touch of European influence. Massive pillars rise before me, intricately inscribed with hieroglyphics and depictions of ancient gods and goddesses.

But I have no time for looking around. As I make my way to the counter, Jasper trots at my heels. Having no plan to enter the museum as a guest, I don't think the dog's presence will be a problem.

"I'm looking for Dr Amelia Fairchild," I inform the receptionist, who looks as ancient as a mummy himself, parchment brown skin and snow-white hair.

"And you are, Ma'am?" he asks in the accented English that I'm becoming quite accustomed to.

"I am Mrs Imogene Lynch from England." Not sure Dr Fairchild is a woman, despite being called Amelia by Mr Banerjee, I decide to keep it neutral. "Dr Fairchild doesn't know me, but if it is no trouble, I'd like to ask the Doctor a question."

The mummy-like receptionist doesn't seem to find my request strange in any way. "Can you wait here, please? I'll see if Miss Fairchild is available." I register the 'miss'. Female, unmarried, or rather, probably married to her job. Quite peculiar to find a female professor, but nothing seems to be too strange here in Cairo.

The poor chap thinks I have some deep archaeological question, no doubt, I think as I watch his back disappear down one of the corridors.

Having no idea what a female academic in 1896 looks like, when I see Dr Amelia Fairchild walking towards me, she reminds me in stature and poise, though not in actual appearance, of my cousin Catherine. That air of a woman of the world, intelligent, sophisticated, liberated from traditional conventions. Standing at 5'6", Amelia Fairchild, similar in height to Cousin Catherine, knows how to carry herself with poise and grace.

I suppose Amelia's slender, yet athletic, build is a testament to the physical demands of her archaeological expeditions. That same sort of muscled wiriness Catherine possesses. They could be sisters though Amelia has auburn hair tied in a practical bun, whereas Cathy's hair is blonde and wispy.

I suppose Catherine knows her, I think as I feel how my face breaks into a smile.

With outstretched hand, Dr Fairchild reaches me. "I

heard you have a question for me, but I didn't catch the name."

"Mrs Imogene Lynch."

"Ah, Mrs Lynch, do come into my office. I'm Amelia Fairchild, as you no doubt know. Just to warn you, my office is a mess, as I've been cleaning some ancient bone structures on my desk."

"Heavens," I can't help observing and she gives me a smile which isn't devoid of some mischief. Captivating emerald-green eyes with a sparkle, take me in with interest. Eyes that are clearly used to analysing her surroundings with meticulous attention to detail. Dr Fairchild's objects of study may be different from mine, but I too have an eye for detail.

"Do you mind if I bring my dog into your office?"

"Not at all, as long as you've got him under control, bones and all you know."

"Absolutely."

Amelia's features are refined, with a well-defined jawline and high cheekbones that add a sense of elegance to her countenance. As she's an attractive lady of about thirty-five, I'm surprised she isn't married.

What mostly puts you at ease around her, apart from her pleasant manners, is her warm smile with a tinge of a mischievous glint, as if she's constantly making a new discovery or solving a particularly challenging riddle of ancient history.

"Come in," she invites me into a spacious office that's crammed with objects. "Don't mind the mess," she repeats.

23

THE BROTHERHOOD OF OSIRIS

Egyptian Museum, the same day, 16 July 1896

'Don't mind the mess' is an understatement to describe Dr Fairchild's space, which has more the air of a laboratory than an office. I now also understand why she insisted I kept Jasper under control. Never before in his ten years and ten months I have seen my dog go so wild in a room.

"Come in, come in," the Egyptologist invites, clearing some scrolls from a chair for me to sit down. "I'm afraid I only have water to offer you as I drink nothing else during work, but it's kept cool in this cupboard here. I can't stand tepid water. What about you, Mrs Lynch?"

"Uh... water will be fine. Thank you," I utter as I look around me in utter surprise meanwhile keeping Jasper's leash as short as possible. He wants to jump against every chair leg and sniff every cupboard and drawer.

"Stop it, Jasper. Sit." He obeys reluctantly, settling at my feet with his nostrils flaring.

And to Dr Fairchild I say, "I'm never seen a more fascinating and mysterious office in my life."

She is busy making space for herself in another chair while the desk is strewn with ancient artefacts, pottery, alabaster jars, sculptures and small figurines of gods and pharaohs. In the midst of this all is an outspread copy of The Times with what it looks like a leg bone and a scalpel. A pair of round glasses and a magnifying glass and some brushes also lie on the newspaper.

"Please never mind my incurable mess," the Egyptologist laughs, waving her arm towards the sturdy wooden shelves with more ancient pottery, ceremonial masks, hieroglyph-covered tablets, and papyrus scrolls.

A considerable portion of her laboratory is also devoted to a collection of scholarly books, journals, and field reports, while encyclopaedias on hieroglyphics, religious practices, history, and the mythology of ancient Egypt are crammed into an overflowing bookcase that spans one of the four walls.

A third wall is dedicated to maps and charts. I see maps of Egypt and the surrounding regions, indicating the various archaeological sites. The maps have hand-drawn annotations and markings indicating important discoveries.

As a reasonable judge of character, I can say with certainty that Dr Fairchild has spent a considerable amount of her time in this office. Maybe as much as on her expeditions.

"Are you done gaping?" She asks with a smile, taking a sip of her water.

"I'm sorry. Is it that obvious?" I make my eyes stop wandering to focus on my host.

"It always causes that reaction in new visitors. I don't even notice this place myself anymore. This is my habitat, but people who step in here for the first time are bound to question my sanity. So, what is it you wanted to know, Mrs Lynch? If I may, you don't have the air of an archaeologist. I can sniff them a mile out, you see." A jingling laughter follows that makes Jasper prick up his ears expectantly.

"You're correct," I answer, with a smile of my own. "I'm only accompanying my cousin..."

Amelia claps two slender hands - that I now see are covered in brown dust - together.

"You are Catherine Lowther's cousin! Of course! How could I have missed that?"

"I am." I say while registering two things: the warmth with which she utters Cathy's name, and the use of Lowther, Cathy's maiden name.

"Oh! How wonderful. Catherine's told me all about you!" Dr Fairchild continues, "you simply must call me Amelia! I feel like I already know you. The smart constable's widow she desperately needed here!"

The emerald eyes take me in with great interest, while I quickly process what she's telling me. Catherine had an ulterior motive to bring me here. Hadn't I thought so? I feel I can be honest with this upfront lady, so I say.

"Do call me Imogene by all means. So, I take it you also know Dr Cornelius Herriot is missing and that it looks like it is serious business?"

"You've come to the right place, Imogene! I think I need you as much as Catherine does. Yes, every hour counts. You'll be wondering why I am not out there trying to find him, and instead sitting here in the dim light scratching an old bone. And honestly, I don't know, either. But, I'm at a loss, and I don't know what I *can* do. The British Museum is sending a London police delegation here, but it will take ages before they arrive and find a way to cooperate with the Egyptian police. By that time poor Cornelius is most likely to be no longer alive."

"Tell me everything from the beginning," I urge her. "There are too many loose ends here."

"How long have you got?" Amelia raises one dark eyebrow.

"As long as it takes," I reply firmly.

"Have you ever heard of an organisation called The Brotherhood of Osiris?"

I shake my head.

"They're basically just bandits with a posh name," Amelia explains, without smiling. "You must know that Osiris was one of the most important Egyptian deities who was associated with the afterlife and resurrection?"

"Yes, that I know." I'm glad not to be totally ignorant.

"These ruffians combine elements of ancient Egyptian mythology with the term 'brotherhood,' which implies they are a secret and closely knit organisation.

"Are they Egyptian or British?" I wonder aloud.

"Egyptian. At least as far as we know. They capture prominent European Egyptologists and archaeologists and hold them hostage. Up till recently they just wanted money in return for the hostage's release, but they've become more radical and nationalist."

"How's that?" I ask, hating the fact I haven't got my notepad with me to write everything down. But never underestimate an intelligent woman sitting across from you.

"Here," she says, handing me a silver-edged small diary and a pencil. "Never mind my scribblings. They're just some early notes I took on this Brotherhood. I would be a useless detective." She shrugs, the smile temporarily reappearing.

"Thank you. Very useful. Go on, please." I immediately write down all Amelia shares with me.

"These men now demand museums abroad the return of Egyptian artefact's they claim are 'stolen' - the Louvre and the British Museum, to name a few. But the reality of the threat sank in last year when Professor Edward Langford disappeared and was never found. Not dead, not alive, just gone. Though the ransom money for his release was ready."

"How horrible," I utter, feeling the hairs on my arms stand up.

"Yes, Professor Langford was a very respected scholar and archaeologist, known for his extensive knowledge of ancient Egyptian history and hieroglyphics. And he was a dear, dear friend. We're such a small circle, us British Egyptologists. We all know each other. Edward is dearly missed."

"I can understand. And what is the position of the Egyptian police in this?"

Suddenly Amelia rises from her chair, wiping a tear from the clear eye.

"Sorry," she says, "Edward loved this office. It's suddenly too much for me. Let's get outside."

"Come, Jasper."

I follow the very straight back of the Egyptologist out of the museum and into the blaring sunlight of the late afternoon.

24

A FRANK TALK WITH CATHERINE

Shepheard's Hotel, later that evening, 16 July 1896

Hours later, when the sun has already dipped beneath the line of the Nile River, I arrive back at Shepheard's Hotel, exhausted and famished, and wondering how to inform Catherine about my visit with her friend.

But I had no need to worry. A scented bath is ready for me, a supper laid out, and Catherine pacing my room in anticipation.

"Oh, you are such a darling," she exclaims, kissing both my cheeks and helping me out of my summer coat. "I've done everything I could to help you relax a little now."

My surprise is considerable. "I assume you know where I was?"

"Yes, yes, of course. I know all the little Ahmeds here in Cairo and one was on the lookout for me all day. I wanted to know where you were. You've never been away this long on your own, Immy. I'm so glad you met Amelia. Isn't she a dear?"

I ease out of my shoes and wriggle my toes. "It's been a long day," I admit. "But a very valuable one at that. Yes, Amelia is...special."

"First you have a bath and then some food and then you have to tell me all about your day." Catherine curls up in one of the chairs and waves an impatient hand at me, "Go, go, into the bath with you."

Coming out half an hour later, refreshed and revitalized, I try to give Cathy an account of my meeting with Amelia, but she keeps interrupting me.

"Why did you never tell *me* you found a fake mummy with Ralph's watch on it?" She wants to know.

"Because I didn't even know at that time that you knew the Herriots."

But that doesn't satisfy my impatient cousin.

"You could have told me when you found out I did."

"Listen Catherine, I know I may sound a little stern now, but one of the things my Thaddeus taught me was not to say too much. I could have told you, yes, but would it have made you feel better? Would it have solved your anxiety? Would you have been able to tell me why it was there?"

Catherine cocks her head, a wrinkle in her forehead.

"Aha," she observes, "so that's how you do it."

"Do what?"

"Be a detective."

"I'm not a detective, Cathy, I'm just a cautious and observant person when things out of the ordinary happen." But I'm glad she doesn't hold it against me that I keep information to myself.

"Oh, go on," she urges me. "Please, may I know everything now?"

I smile at her remark. "At this moment, yes, but I cannot guarantee I will always disclose every step along the way. I won't when I fear more eyes and ears on the matter will muddle the waters, so to say. But I'll never keep anything from you because I don't trust you."

"I know that, Immy. Now what did Amelia and you decide to do about this Brotherhood of Osiris?"

"There's little we can do right now," I say cautiously. "We're not even sure it's them who kidnapped Cornelius. There is no trace so far. The Brotherhood hasn't contacted the British Museum yet. At least as far as Amelia knows. They usually contact the archaeologist's employer to demand the ransom. But the British Museum didn't want to wait for that demand, so they sent a Scotland Yard delegation with the anticipated ransom amount on its way this week. The officers are supposed to arrive in a couple of weeks."

Catherine looked pained.

"Weeks?"

"Listen Cathy," I say softly. "We don't know for sure Cornelius is kidnapped, and maybe not by them. He could have just disappeared by himself."

"Or had an accident," she adds bitterly.

"When was the last time you saw him?" It's my time to ask questions now.

"Last year." A deep sigh escapes Catherine's breath. "I knew via Eddy that he was going to be back in Egypt around this time but also that he was next on the list to be captured by the Brotherhood. Amelia must have told you about the list these crooks distributed?"

I nod.

"That's why I was so nervous all the time," Catherine continues, and then a little sheepishly, "and I wanted you to be here with me. Because you're good at solving these things and you're always so level-headed. Of course, the Brotherhood has taken Cornelius hostage, but you saw him only a couple of days ago here in the hotel, though you thought it was his brother Ralph. I still have hopes we can get him out of their claws. We don't have to wait for Scotland Yard, Immy. I brought enough money in banknotes with me to buy the entire Shepheard's Hotel if needed, so that will certainly be enough to buy free my C"

"Catherine," I gasp, "you did what?!" I shudder at the idea my cousin is carrying so much money on her. I don't even want to know how much. Or where she got it.

"Yes, that was the other reason I was a little ill at ease. But it's in the hotel's safe now so I sleep fine as far as that stack of banknotes is concerned."

"Cathy?" I look at her straight. "Did Cornelius ever tell you if he thought his wife would be able to do him harm? That she wanted a divorce, or something?"

"Why are you asking that?" Catherine looks puzzled and the wrinkle is back in her forehead. "I don't think so. I mean I was unprepared for her escorting him to Egypt, but I don't think they were at each other's throats. Just grown apart and as you now know, she is in love with his twin brother."

"I will have to talk with her tomorrow," I say. "I really need to get that nagging thought out of my head that she has something to do with it."

Catherine nods. "Just keep me out of it, please."

"Of course. You don't have to meet her if you don't want to but there might come a point in the next few days that the two of you will encounter one another. After all, Cornelius is still her legal husband."

Then I change the subject to another matter on my mind. "Amelia told me that both she and Sir Edmund Worthington are also on the Brotherhood's list. Thank God, you're not on it, Catherine."

"I know. That's why Amelia mainly stays at the Museum here in Cairo and Eddy only does the tours at Giza. They're too afraid to do excavations now, which is a shame as there so much that still needs digging up and the tools to do that are getting better and more precise by the day. Everyone involved in Egyptian archaeology is afraid these days. I think that's exactly the purpose of this Brotherhood."

"It may be," I agree. "But now we need to get some sleep."

"I'll try." Catherine gets up to go to her own quarters, "but I find sleep quite evasive these nights."

25

A SCHEMING LOVER ON A MISSION

Shepheard's Hotel, the next morning, 17 July 1896

After a fitful night of sleep in which I dreamt I was tied to the back of a donkey cart and had been dragged off into the pitch-black night of the Sahara desert, I wake up in my crisp and lavender-scented bed at the Shepheard's hotel in Cairo. It may not be under my flowery eiderdown in Honeydew Mansion, but I'm safe. My nightmare an illusionary part of the realm of the night.

It tells me, though, I might be getting too involved in the case of Cornelius's disappearance. *Always keep a healthy distance from the case, my dear*. That is my wise benedict talking to me.

"What is it with the Lowthers that I have to unravel their complicated relationships through trials and tribulations of my own? First Finley and now Catherine," I ask Roly-Poly, who snores lightly and yaps in his sleep, certainly not at Egyptian bandits but more likely at rabbits in the tall grass around Tiversack Lake.

For a moment I yearn for home, the thick grey rain clouds over the lake, my wonderful flower and kitchen garden. Mrs. Peaton singing arias in the kitchen and Doctor Rule coming around the backdoor for a cuppa and a chat. Life seems so easy and uneventful in Landdulton. But I'm not one to lament and do nothing. I have an obligation to help my cousin in any way I can.

As long as you don't put yourself in danger, my benedict seems to whisper to me.

"I know," I say aloud, not caring should anyone hear me talk to myself. "This is a strange and perhaps dangerous country, but I have two knowledgeable female escorts, Dr Amelia and Cousin Catherine, who are here to guide me through the mazes of the Egyptian underworld."

CATHERINE IS out as usual before breakfast, and I have a strong inkling she spends her early hours with her friend Amelia. I had never known my cousin to be such an early riser, but she is up hours before my half seven alarm clock. After a quick breakfast in my room, I knock on Mrs Herriot's door. Then listen. Nothing. Just when I want to turn on my heels, I hear the door creak.

"Mrs Lynch?" The voice is sleepy, almost drugged.

"Yes, it's me, Mrs Herriot. Apologies for having awakened you."

"No, it's no trouble. Please come in and forgive my night clothes. I only manage some sleep in the morning but do come in. Would you care for some tea, or coffee perhaps?" Winnifred's voice is slurred. I assume she's been taking laudanum to sleep. I've heard that tone of voice and seen the veiled eyes before.

"I'm fine, thank you. I just breakfasted," I say, taking a chair in the shaded room that smells as if it hasn't been aired for weeks.

"I have some news about Dr Corne...," I begin, but Winnifred doesn't let me finish my sentence, waves a weary arm.

"Please, Mrs Lynch. Let me explain. I should have days ago but both Herriot brothers urged me to keep my mouth shut. I can't any longer."

Oh no, my mind thinks, *oh no!*

Just that. It's going to be even more complicated.

"Go ahead," I say, trying to not sound too dispirited.

She hesitates, clears her throats.

"I agreed to accompany Cornelius on this trip with a bad thought in mind. Mind you, Ralph is innocent. He knows nothing about this. It was only me. It's not that I hate Cornelius, I just don't love him. Never have. And I want to be able to marry Ralph, you see."

I nod, thinking *blow the gaff, Mrs Herriot.*

"Of course, I heard about this gang, The Brotherhood of Osiris. Though I'm not living with Cornelius, we do correspond. He told me about the threat they were under as Egyptologists, also in case he might be captured and held ransom -· or worse! - what would happen to me as his widow. And that's when I got this idea in my head..." She stops again, looks at me almost pleadingly.

"You haven't...yourself...?" I asked sternly.

"Oh, no no!" she waves her hands. "What do you take me for, Mrs Lynch?"

I have no clue, I think but don't say. *You tell me what you are, Winnifred Herriot.*

"I did want to get Cornelius out of the way. I thought I'd find a way when I was here. I'd never been to Cairo before, so I thought I would find a hired killer on every street corner." She swallows hard, then adds softly, "I had no idea what I was thinking. It took being away from Dartmond to open my eyes that I had been obsessive about marrying for love. I was shocked to find I had entertained the thought of hiring someone to kill my husband only for that. Cornelius has never been anything but kind and polite with me. We're just not in love. I think he's in love with someone else, but I don't know. He never talks of another woman in his life."

That I do know, I think, but again not say. I will not give a person with such a vile mind the pleasure of telling her she is right and the person her husband is in love with is under the same roof as her.

"But he knows of you and Ralph?" I ask.

"Yes, of course."

"And does Cornelius hold that against his brother?"

The first real smile glides over her pretty face. "No, not at all, they've always been close, you know, as twin brothers. Alike on the outside but very different inside."

"And does Ralph hold it against his brother that he is married to you and preventing Ralph from being able to?"

"Gosh, Mrs Lynch, you really sound like a police officer now, interrogating me like this." She quips.

"This is no joke, Mrs Herriot, please answer my question." I can hear Thaddeus's authority in my own voice.

"Sometimes," Winnifred answers reluctantly. "That's why I didn't want him involved in my ...uh ... little scheme."

"It's not 'a little scheme' to concoct plans to hire out the murder of your husband. It's revolting." Her playful innocence irks me. "What made you change your mind?"

Winnifred seems to sober up as I confront her head-on.

"Immediately after we arrived at the Shepheard's Hotel, I saw the idiocy of it all. Maybe it was already on our voyage here. I just couldn't make any real plans or approach people. But somehow Cornelius, who's bright as a button as you can imagine, got an idea of what had been in my head and that's when he played the pranks on me, until..."

Her voice trails off.

"I'm innocent, Mrs Lynch. I have nothing to do with Cornelius's disappearance. I swear it on all that's holy. I'm innocent."

Do I believe her? A scheming lover on a mission of murder for hire...?

26

THE ARCHAEOLOGIST, THE LOVER
AND THE DETECTIVE

Egyptian Museum, Cairo, the afternoon of the same day, 17 July 1896

As I make my way to the Egyptian museum on another clear blue summer's day in Cairo, I am still reeling from the stupidity and short-sightedness of women like Winnifred. They have it all and want more. Well not only women, I correct myself, mankind can be short-sighted. And I'm no exception to the human race.

In a way I am relieved, as I do believe in Winnifred's innocence. And she gave me a few necessary answers. Firstly, Cornelius was responsible for the pranks of the fake mummy and the four-hour fake kidnapping of Winnifred. Secondly, and more seriously, he's most likely in the hands of the Brotherhood of Osiris. Because of that conclusion, I'm on my way to Amelia. With my Roly-Poly following me as usual.

I find Amelia and Catherine deeply absorbed in study

over the bones of the pharaoh's leg on Amelia's desk. The auburn and blonde heads close together. No talking, just concentrated work with scalpel and brush.

For a moment I stand in the doorway, not wanting to interrupt their pleasant moment of carefree togetherness being the bringer of bad tidings. Amelia spots me first.

"Ah, Madame Detective." Her elegant face lights up, the emerald-green eyes twinkling.

"Don't call me that," I reply with a smile.

"Immy?" Catherine looks up surprised. "What are you doing here?"

"Wrong question, Cath," Amelia beams. "When Imogene arrives it means there is news."

"There is," I say with a sigh. "But it doesn't mean there is a solution. Only more questions."

I lay out for the archaeologist and the lover what Winnifred Herriot disclosed to me. Both are horrified at the wife's initial plans, but I warn against a witch hunt.

"For what it's worth, I believe in her innocence. Of course, I can't stake my life on it but based on my experience with criminals and from the brief moments I saw them together, plus her reaction after his disappearance and the remorse she just showed, I think we need to give her the benefit of the doubt. Which leaves us..."

A knock on the door interrupts me. A stricken museum clerk sticks his head around the door.

"Telegram for you Dr Fairchild. It's...it's from the Brotherhood of Osiris.

"For me?" I see the brave academic sway on her legs for a moment. "Shouldn't it be for the British Museum or for Dr Malik Abdalla, the director here?"

"It says Dr Amelia Fairchild." The stricken clerk puts

the flimsy blue paper on her desk and rushes out as if the devil's on his heels. All three of us stare at the telegram. I'm sure our eyes are big as saucers and our hearts beat like hammers.

"You want me to open it?" I ask, braving myself.

"It will be in Arabic. You won't be able to read it," Amelia replies as her hand slowly creeps to the paper.

"Oh no," Catherine moans, "dear God, don't tell me C is dead!"

Meet at Ruins of Ibn-Razek. Stop.
Midnight 17 July. Stop. Bring 10,000 EGP.
Stop. Come alone. Shadow of Osiris. Stop.

AMELIA TRANSLATES the contents of the telegram and I understand she must read and perhaps speak fluent Arabic. She immediately presses the telegram into my hands, as if I'm the expert on deciphering its authenticity. I can make nothing of the Arabic alphabet, but I can see this message is real. And it's urgent.

"Do you have that amount of money, Cathy?" I demand, "how much is that in British pounds?"

"Over 2000 GBP," Amelia calculates quickly.

Catherine is too stupefied to answer, then stutters, "shouldn't... shouldn't we involve the police? Amelia, there's no way you're going to that deserted place on your own at midnight. It's a trap to catch you as well. It's a trap," she yammers again.

"What is the location like?" I ask, trying to stay level-headed now that we seem to be coming into a rapid.

"It's an ancient archaeological site about four miles east of Cairo. It has some mysterious ruins, half-excavated in recent years," Amelia explains.

"I have the money," Catherine seems to recover from her stupor. "That Shadow doesn't know your face, Amelia. It's my money, so I'm going to hand it over."

"Cath, no!' Amelia protests. "I don't want to be difficult, but my Arabic is better than yours. And we want that transaction to be as swift and smooth as possible."

"As far as I understand from your translation, Amelia, The Shadow of Osiris doesn't state the Brotherhood will actually liberate Dr Cornelius. Is that correct? He doesn't even say it is *for* Cornelius," I intervene in their squabbles over who will hand over the ransom.

Amelia studies the telegram again. "You're right. It's not there."

"We can't contact them back to check. And bandits don't take kindly to being checked anyway," I observe drily. "We have no other choice but to involve the police. It's too dangerous to go out there alone and unarmed."

"But it's a wide terrain of nothing around those ruins," Amelia explains. "You couldn't hide a policeman there unless you buried him entirely in the sand."

"We're not doing this without a police escort," I declare.

27

UNEXPECTED HELP FROM HOME

En route for the Ruins of Ibn-Razek, evening of 17 July 1896

"Promise me you won't tell Winnifred Herriot anything about tonight," Catherine urges me as we make our way to the Shepheard's Hotel to change into dark clothes and prepare for a long evening and night.

Though Catherine and I aren't supposed to accompany Amelia to the Ruins at midnight, the three of us have decided that Catherine and I will be waiting together with Inspector Pasha and his men at a low stone wall some mile away from the ruins.

If anything goes wrong during the transaction or Amelia is taken as well, Inspector Pasha will not hesitate to intervene.

"It's risky business, ladies," the black-moustached inspector had remarked with a heaviness in his voice. "One wrong move and it may turn to violence."

I am all too aware of that. And of keeping Winnifred Herriot out of it all. *Should I really do this, Thaddeus, or have I gone mad?* I ask, studying the police officer across from me, who - despite the distance and the different culture - greatly reminds me of my late husband. There is a tranquil safety around Inspector Pasha and a respectful attitude that women can have a role in solving crimes, but that he will protect me. I nod, knowing I'm probably about to do the most insane thing in my life, but Thaddeus doesn't seem to contradict me on this.

With as much courage as I can muster, I say, "Don't worry, cousin. Winnifred will only be told the basics when Cornelius is safely back at the hotel. Inshallah, if God or Allah wants it."

I'm glad my Will is drawn-up and safely tucked away at *Messrs Ephraim Galway & Lambert Watson, Solicitors* in Landdulton. In case anything happens to me tonight, which I pray won't be the case. My direct worries are about Jasper. He was supposed to go to Mrs Peaton should anything happen to me, but I haven't arranged for his transport back to England yet. I write a quick note that I put in the top drawer on my cabinet in my hotel room.

Should the circumstances occur that I pass away in Cairo before my dog Jasper, I hereby leave the amount of 100EGP for my dog's transfer to England + the fare for a keeper. Jasper should only be delivered into the hands of my housekeeper Mrs Peaton, at Honeydew Mansion, Landdulton, The Cotswolds, England.

Mrs Imogene Lynch

I TUCK the note and the money in an envelope and feel lighter having completed that important action. Jasper isn't too keen to be left alone all evening, but I give him extra care and a piece of sausage he loves and after that he goes to sleep peacefully on his cushion in my room.

It is with a heavy heart I leave that room an hour later to see an equally grave-looking Catherine wait for me in the hall.

"Ready?" I ask as we walk on soft-soled shoes to wait for the carriage that will take as to the dunes two miles from the ruins, which we will continue to on foot.

"As ready as one can be," she sighs. In a moment of candour adds, "oh Immy, I should never have drawn you into this but you're the only one I know who handles this with such composure."

"Only on the outside, cousin, my insides are all in a knot."

Half an hour later, two carriages leave the Cairo police headquarters. Catherine, Amelia and I are seated together in one carriage guarded by two heavily armed Egyptian police officers that squeeze in beside us. The other carriage is for Inspector Pasha and his team.

"Wait, we're here!"

We hear a loud cry in a very British accent and all gaze in surprise out of the carriage window into the failing daylight.

The stagecoach from Alexandria filled with at least six or seven Scotland Yard men comes to a screeching halt outside the police station. The Bobbies in tropical uniforms but still sporting their black helmets, hang out of the windows, while their commander, a tall, thin man with a drooping moustache and stern looking eyes, exchanges the stagecoach for a place in Inspector Pasha's carriage. The entire convoy of, now three, carriages pulled by horses sets off to the eastern part of Cairo for the first stretch of our journey.

"Amazing timing," Amelia states quietly, "I feel a lot better now."

"So do I," Catherine and I say at the same time. The arrival of the Scotland Yard officers will be a great help to the Egyptian force when we come face to face with the Brotherhood of Osiris and things don't work out as planned.

I think I'm the only one of the ladies who realizes such a large crowd of policemen can also make the bandits balk. Will there be enough space to hide them all out of sight? That's a matter for the Scotland Yard commander and Inspector Pasha to solve.

Meanwhile I study Amelia, who must inwardly be consumed by nerves. She doesn't show it though. She looks calm and composed in a black men's suit that is too big for her small frame. She insisted on trousers so she could move faster than if she was hampered by long skirts and petticoats.

"I wonder if the British Museum sent money as well?" Catherine muses. "I wouldn't mind spending my own 10,000 on something other than a gang of bandits."

"Of course the British Museum didn't send the bobbies empty-handed," Amelia assures her, and then adds with a grin, "I hope the case I have to hand over to them is embossed with Her Majesty's seal. That would teach those scoundrels."

I'm not exactly sure if anything would teach scoundrels anything but I keep quiet and try to make out the landscape in the quickly falling night. The horses, though used to pulling carriage through the sand, struggle with their heavy loads and we progress slowly.

According to Amelia's maps, the Ruins of Ibn-Razek lay on the outskirts of Cairo. It's a place steeped in legends and shrouded in mystery. She told me there is even a persistent rumour the ancient Pharaohs themselves cursed the land, and that those who dared trespass upon it would awaken long-forgotten spirits seeking vengeance.

Though I don't believe in these heathen spells, I must say that what I can discern outside is spooky indeed.

And the full moon rises over the horizon, oversized and orange and ominous. I feel myself praying the Lord Our Father, over and over again.

28

THE SCARIEST NIGHT OF MY LIFE

The Ruins of Ibn-Razek, late night, 17 July 1896

My chain watch tells me it's about 11pm when we're all in our designated places and Amelia is about to set out with her heavy leather bag containing the 10,000 Egyptian pounds demanded by The Shadow. It's as if even the full moon, hanging high in the cloud-covered sky and casting an eerie glow over the desolate ruins, is holding its breath.

I barely dare to watch Amelia's brave, slender figure cautiously making her way across the sand towards the crumbling structures. The air is thick with the scent of sand and ancient decay, and a spine-chilling wind whistles through the crevices of the aged stones nearby.

The rest of the surroundings are still, as if struck by death. Nothing hints at the men lying behind the wall alongside Catherine and me, while others have crept to the other side of the ruins to guard the back entrance. Though I've understood no one knows from where the

Brotherhood will emerge, making it all the more necessary to hide men and carriages and horses out of sight in the nearby bushes.

"It's a gamble," the Scotland Yard commander, who'd introduced himself as Chief Superintendent Alexander Cromwell, had grumbled. "But we'll have to roll with it." Then the tall and wiry chief superintendent had put some extra wax in his already stiff moustache tips as if ready to impale The Shadow on them.

I feel my heart pounding as I lie alongside Catherine flat on my stomach while holding her hand, that shakes as the leaf on a windblown tree. The night is still hot and dry, and the warm wind doesn't help to cool us. I feel perspiration form on my forehead but don't dare to take out my white handkerchief to wipe it away. We cannot talk either, not even whisper, as voices carry a long way in the desert. So, we lie and wait. Motionless, menaced, mindful.

Amelia has reached the ruins. Her lantern flickers, casting eerie shadows that dance along the walls. I feel myself having difficulty breathing. *How can she be so brave in the eye of so much danger?* I think as I peer through the holes in the stone wall.

"The spirits of the long-gone pharaohs will guide my every move," she'd said with a dry smile. "I've invested so much in them. Now they must do something in return."

I doubt that any help from dead pharaohs will help poor Amelia. Her only hope is the heavily armed policemen that follow her every move here on earth.

The hands on my clock creep far too slowly. I can see them illuminated in the dim light of the moon. Then we hear a low, haunting chant echoing through the ruins. I peer and peer and then see them. Cloaked in dark robes, five figures, emerging from the shadows, one of them hanging in between two of the dark-cloaked men. That must be Cornelius. I feel Catherine stir next to me. She clamps one hand over her mouth, clearly to refrain from crying out.

I breathe through my teeth. *Good work officers*, I think admiringly. The Brotherhood approaches from the one side that was left open. Pure chance, of course, but a first small victory. Unseen officers are possibly closing that entrance that will most likely also be their exit now.

I fix my eyes on the one who must be The Shadow of Osiris - the man in the centre, taller and broader than the rest. The glow from the moon outlines his sinister silhouette as he approaches Amelia. I try to see any weaponry as Thaddeus taught me to, but if they possess any – and I don't doubt that - they hide it well. For the likes of them, I suppose knives in boots and guns under the cloaks. All we can do is count on our policemen being more heavily armed than them. And our superior position enabling us to watch them while they are unaware of the armed forces that Amelia brought in her wake.

The two men holding Cornelius stay at a short distance but are clearly visible between the ruins.

"God help Amelia and Cornelius," I pray.

THE NEGOTIATIONS between the bandit and the female Egyptologist must be under way but I can see she's still holding onto the bag, her lantern illuminating the side of her face and the bag in her hand. It's as if the entire desert night holds its breath.

Suddenly a haunting, ethereal wail fills the air, and the ground beneath the people at the ruins seems to shake. I feel my blood curl and think I will die for fear on the spot. It is as if unseen eyes watch from the darkness, and make the ruins come alive with malevolent spirits.

Amelia stands still like a statue. Oh, how I admire her strength. The two black figures holding Dr Cornelius release him and he sinks as a lump into the sand, lying still. More dead than alive. The ritual that now follows leaves me confused, but I do understand the tremendous value of an Egyptologist like Dr Fairchild, who does know what to do.

The Shadow's four accomplices stay back, forming a semi-circle around the Shadow, who is now next to the collapsed Cornelius and standing 20 feet away from Amelia, facing her. For a moment, time seems to stand still, and I worry we are stuck, that the exchange cannot happen. Then, the Shadow walks around the circle clock-wise in slow, menacing steps towards Amelia. I can see his white teeth flash in the moonlight as he grins at Amelia.

Amelia, meanwhile, has dropped the bag of money in the sand and also walks clockwise around the circle, always staying exactly opposite the Shadow, facing him the entire time. At one point, Amelia, the Shadow, Cornelius and the money formed a clock face, spread across 12, 3, 6, and 9 o'clock. And the Shadow's men just stand in the distance, ominous with black cloaks flapping in the rapidly cooling desert air, but still no weapons drawn. It appears the Brotherhood is actually going to honour the exchange and no double-cross will transpire.

A deadly silence but for the incessant desert wind and the soft moaning of the body on the ground. The Shadow howls again – now it is clear the earlier ethereal wail was him - and both he and Amelia dive for their desired parcels. Amelia immediately slumps to the ground to tend to C. and check he is okay, while the Shadow grabs the bag and runs towards his men.

Partway to his men, there is a clunk and the Shadow stops and shakes the bag. Then he turns to face Amelia across the sand, tears the bag open, dumping it out on the sand. A few notes fall out, and then rocks tumble to the ground. I shiver to my very core at the voice that tears through the night, it is spine-chilling, and my heart wants to stop.

"The curse of Ibn-Razek will follow you and your damned country for eternity," Catherine translates the words for me, breaking the silence behind the wall while she shivers all-over.

The next moments happen as in a flash. Before the last words of the curse leave his mouth, Amelia's lantern is extinguished, and it becomes dark between the ruins. My eyes need a moment to adjust to only the light of the moon again. I peer and faintly see Cornelius moving, reaching out an arm in Amelia's direction. The two lonesome figures sneak away from the ruins and struggle in our direction while the Shadow furiously throws rocks about, presumably double-checking that there really is no money in the bag.

"The real curse of Ibn-Razek is the Brotherhood of Osiris," Inspector Pasha shouts through his megaphone.

"Lay down your weapons, Shadow. All of you, lay down your weapons."

From everywhere, Egyptians and British officers appear and close in on the bandits. Shots ring, bodies fall, and the desert sand flies everywhere. It even enters my ears and nose.

"Lie down," I shout to Catherine who tries to scramble to her feet and run. With force, I keep her pinned to the ground. From the corners of my eyes, I see Superintendent Cromwell has reached Amelia and Cornelius and brings them to safety behind the wall, next to us. Then I don't look up anymore but keep my head down. I've seen enough. Catherine sobs in my arms but doesn't raise herself anymore.

"Sorry for hurting you," I murmur, and then I add in an uncommon cry of desperation from my side, "dear God, let none of the good guys be harmed."

THEN SILENCE REIGNS again and our ordeal is over.

29

THE PECULIAR VANISHING ACT OF
MR RALPH HERRIOT

*On our way back from the Ruins to Cairo, early
morning 18 July 1896*

When I raise my head again and hold the shivering Catherine in my arms, I see Amelia and Cornelius being giving a drink from a flask, while Superintendent Cromwell and Inspector Hamdi Pasha gather all the men around them.

"We've killed all five of them, including the one who called himself the Shadow," Cromwell booms.

"Only one British officer lightly wounded in his hand," Pasha chimes in. A sigh of relief goes through everyone.

"Now bring our British guests to their carriage and escort them back to their hotel,' the Egyptian police officer orders his men. "Superintendent Cromwell and a delegation of the Egyptian and British officers will stay here at the Ruins of Ibn-Razek to collect all the evidence and take the bodies to the morgue for identification. Hurry up and make sure you send a doctor to Shepheard's to examine Mr Herriot."

Thus, we're bundled off to our carriage, feeling discordant and disoriented. In the safety of the carriage, we eye one another as if almost shy in each other's company.

There is a strained silence. Glances, more glances. Bewilderment.

"But you're not Cornelius!" Catherine and Amelia stammer at the same time.

"Who said I was?" The man in the crumpled suit with matted black hair and a fresh jab on his swollen face, says with difficulty. "I'm Ralph Herriot. That stupid Brotherhood took the wrong man." He rests his weary, bruised head against the cushions and shuts his eyes with difficulty.

We're as still as the wind that has died outside. I try to think but the cogwheels of my brain refuse to work.

Then almost in a whisper, Ralph adds, "I think they took me for my brother. At least that's what I pieced together from their garbled talk. Kept prodding me and asking me about Ramses II. They became really rough when I couldn't answer any of their questions. Just as well I'm not my famous brother. It cost me some bruises and a concussion but they're none the wiser. And now they are dead." He's silent for a moment, has difficulty breathing, then adds, "Thank you for saving me. This was for sure the most perilous experience in my whole life, but as the eldest brother I took it gladly for Corny."

It's unclear if Ralph Herriot has a peculiar sense of

humour even under the circumstances or if he's serious. I know I shouldn't ask him questions in his current condition, but the investigator gets the better of me.

"Since when are you in Egypt, Mr Herriot? The last I heard from Mayor Banerjee, you were in Dartmond?"

"About a week, I guess. I immediately came out here when Cornelius told me he would finally divorce Winnifred. I wanted to surprise her and take her back home to Dartmond. Well, what a surprise!" He answers with his eyes closed. Alright, he *is* a humorous man making the best of his lamentable situation. Or maybe it's the shock that makes him relativise his situation.

"Is Winnifred still here?" he suddenly opens his eyes, looking anxious. Amelia and Catherine have fallen silent, clearly unable to grasp this unexpected turn of events.

"Yes, she's safe and well at the Shepheard's," I reassure him. "She will be very happy to see you. And pray tell me, where *is* your brother?"

"As far as I know he's still in Dartmond where I left him two weeks' ago, filing for the divorce."

"But your brother was here a month ago?"

"Mrs Lynch, you ask way too many questions of a bruised man, but the answer is yes. Cornelius originally came here with Winnifred, but when he was sure she wanted the divorce as well, he wired me to tell me she was all mine, and he would separate from her."

The cogwheels slowly gain momentum. Winnifred *is* innocent. Then I look at Catherine. This is good news for her as well. Not only is Cornelius not in danger, but he will also be a single man soon. But Catherine's teeth clatter and she seems unable to understand what's going on around her. Amelia, who showed the courage of a lioness just now at the Ruins, does comprehend the entire picture and takes in Ralph with a bemused look on her face.

"How and where did the Brotherhood catch you?" she demands.

He utters a dry laugh, coughs up some grey sand. "Immediately after I descended from the train in Cairo. Nice little welcome. I had no idea what was going on. For a moment I thought my brother was playing a prank, just like we used to do as kids, but this was dead serious, and it was a long week."

Ralph opens weary eyes and fixes them on Amelia. "Thank you," he says, grabbing her hand warmly, "thank you for being so fearless. I don't know if I'd have had the guts had I been in your shoes.'

"Well, I rescued the wrong man, didn't I?"

"Yes," Ralph replies with honesty. "I'm not half the worth of my brother but I'm glad you didn't know."

I wonder why I thought Ralph Herriot was a vain and pompous man. He is warm, down-to-earth, and honest. I hope he and Winnifred will be very happy together.

Catherine seems to revive when the hotel come into view. "Let's wake Winnifred and offer Ralph a welcome drink."

"He should see that doctor first," I remark.

Ralph fixes his swollen eyes on Catherine and with a crooked smile says, "I'm so glad I finally have a face to the name. Cornelius has talked so warmly of you, Mrs Northwind."

Ouch, I think, *will Stafford ever let Catherine go, like Cornelius has agreed to let Winnifred go?*

I can see it in her face, and I squeeze her hand.

"Thank you," she says stiffly.

"Don't despair," he emboldens her, "the times are changing."

30

OUR LAST DAY IN CAIRO

Cairo, two weeks later, 1 August 1896

As you can expect the past weeks have been quite eventful. First Catherine and I needed to recuperate from our arduous adventure at the Ruins of Ibn-Razek and then we had to decide whether we wanted to stay and continue our Egypt visit or rather go home, so Catherine can meet up with Cornelius.

I'm now sitting in my room at the Shepheard's with a new telegram from Mayor Banerjee in my hands and Jasper at my feet.

Sincere apologies mistaking Dr C. Herriot for Mr R. Herriot. Stop. Glad all are safe. Stop. Do visit when back. Mayor B. Stop.

I HAD FELT it my duty to inform the kind mayor it was Cornelius he'd seen in Dartmond and in the same message I had let him know Ralph was safe.

For a moment I gaze out over the Nile River wondering to what extent this ancient country has also gotten into my own bones. Though I'll never aspire to becoming an Egyptologist, spending a lot of time among them in the past weeks - Sir Edmund and Amelia often joined Catherine and me - and listening to their lively conversations, I can understand the fascination with other cultures and religions.

I'm just not a scholar. I don't have that kind of brain. They solve other puzzles than I do, though I feel I've not been up to the task of helping Catherine as I should have. But then again, a dangerous gang of Egyptian bandits isn't even something my Thaddeus would have burnt his fingers on.

But in essence, the Brotherhood of Osiris was a lot of fluff. They were Cairo local criminals, petty thieves, and burglars, not the secret ancient association out to restore Egypt's glory days as they had pretended to be.

Ralph told us they were quite panicky when they found out he didn't speak a word of Arabic and kept pointing at his chest, repeating '*Ralph* Herriot'.

Oh, I'm daydreaming again. Winnifred and Ralph are as happy as two lambs in the meadow and left for England a week ago. I promised I would drop by when back in England. Strange how one gets to know people in a different way when abroad and certainly under such extraordinary circumstances.

"Immy, are you coming? Amelia wants to help us choose souvenirs for home. And I need to have the artifacts I promised to bring back to the British Museum packed and shipped." Catherine knocks on my door and enters before I can say 'yes.' This trip and our adventure has brought us much closer as well. She looks pretty in her scarlet dress, her blonde hair half hidden by a large hat, white lace gloves and matching parasol. Her face is smooth and unwrinkled again. She can't wait to get back to England, and to Cornelius.

I attach Jasper's leash to his collar and rise from my chair.

"You look lovely," I say, putting my arm through hers.

"All your doing, sweet cousin," she says warmly. And I must confess I'm glad she feels I played a role in her resurrection.

"Today marks the end of our sojourn in Cairo, Cathy," I say rather melancholically as we descend the steps of the Shepheard's Hotel for almost the final time.

"Oh, dear cousin, I cannot help but feel a mix of excitement and nostalgia, too. I think we're excellent travel companions. We should travel together more often."

I smile at her kind offer. "You'll soon be out here with Cornelius again and have no need for me, Cathy."

"Nonsense. I love you, Immy. I want us to remain close as we used to be as children and are now again."

"So do I, Cathy. You're like a sister to me."

The sun rises higher over the Nile, casting a golden glow over the city I have come to love, as if the sun embraces the beauty of this ancient land one last time. We embark on a leisurely stroll through the bustling streets of Cairo, our light summer skirts billowing gently in the warm breeze.

We watch as the locals go about their daily chores, and let our nostrils be caressed by the aroma of exotic spices. Merchants display their vibrantly coloured wares and enticing scents. Camels and donkeys pass by, carrying goods from far-off lands, a sight that never ceases to amaze me.

As if our steps are synchronized, we find ourselves at the Egyptian Museum and knock on Amelia Fairchild's door. But then we see the note she left for us on the table.

Dear Catherine and Imogene,

Edmund and I will come for a farewell dinner at the hotel tonight. We're out in the fields again, now it's safe. Such bliss. Have a lovely day and don't forget to drop by at Mahmoud's shop at the Khan El Khalili Market. My presents for you are all wrapped up and waiting for you there.

See you tonight, Yours Amelia.

"I CAN'T BLAME HER," Catherine says when she sees my disappointed face. "They need these days when the light is still strong, Immy. They've lost so much time doing field work when these stupid bandits wrecked their schedule."

"You're right," I agree, "and we'll see them tonight.

Cathy and I wander through the museum one more

time, losing ourselves in the enigmatic world of antiquities. We marvel at the display of relics, the statues of pharaohs, and the hieroglyph-covered scrolls. Catherine is a wonderful guide, able to recount the tales of a civilization long gone, and my heart swells with wonder at her knowledge and passion. I too find solace in the museum's hallowed halls, captivated by its history. The dark side of our quest lain to rest.

As the sun climbs higher, we make our way one more time to the Khan El Khalili bazaar, to find Mahmoud's stall and have lunch. We weave through the maze of stalls, where merchants bargain with customers over delicate trinkets and intricate jewellery, glittering with lapis lazuli and golden scarabs. Vibrant fabrics and shimmering silks catch my eye, and I can't help myself. Both Cathy and I purchase a few yards of the same silk as keepsakes of our time together in this enchanting city.

At lunchtime, we dip into a charming café we've been in before, where I now know Cathy tried to get more information about her C from the locals. We sip fragrant mint tea and indulge in delectable local delicacies that melt on my tongue.

"You've definitely given me back my appetite, Catherine," I say as I share a sugared pastry with Jasper.

"I'm glad I did something back for you, Immy. You needed to eat more. Everyone could see that."

"I'm not getting fat, am I?" I ask in fear.

"Don't be silly. You're slim as a lily," Catherine rhymes. I listen with pleasure to the hum of conversations in Arabic around us and am proud I can catch a few words here and there. Other languages fill the air as well. This lively metropolis is a symphony of cultures, something I suddenly realize I will miss in Landdulton. There is something comforting and inspiring to be part of a melting pot of traditions.

"LET's take a felucca ride along the Nile," Catherine cheers, "with all our rigmaroles we haven't even been boating."

I love being on river water that is flat and smooth as marble. No seasickness for me here. The boat glides gracefully through the tranquil waters, giving us a magnificent view of Cairo's skyline. We keep saying, "oh and ahh," and pointing out buildings to each other. The minarets and domes of the mosques in particular stand tall against the sky, creating a timeless panorama. I'll never forget the enchantment I felt while my eyes feasted on this *Crown of the Wild*.

As the day wanes, Catherine and I return to the Shepheard's Hotel for our very last night, laden with parcels for home and our senses filled to the brim as with a vivid dream.

"Let's eat on the hotel's rooftop tonight," Catherine suggests. "It's just that kind of summer evening for being high up and having a last view of the city's panorama by night."

Amelia and Sir Edmund join us as we're seated at the best table to see the sun begin its last Egyptian descent for us. The sky is painted with hues of pink and orange, and the call to prayer echoes through the air. The majestic Pyramids of Giza loom in the distance, guardians of a timeless legacy and a heart-stopping adventure for us. We even glance towards the Ruins of Ibn-Razek and heave a sigh of relief.

"To friendship," we toast.

"To Egypt," I say, "the country that brought us together and made us friends again."

"To Egypt," we toast.

My heart aches to leave this captivating place, but the memories I have gathered will remain etched in my soul forever. And so, as the day ends, I retire to my room, where my trunk awaits my return to England.

Egypt and Cairo in particular, have left an indelible mark on me. As I lay down to sleep, I am filled with gratitude for the extraordinary adventure this country has bestowed upon me—a treasure and friendships to cherish for all the days of my life.

31

C & C

London, 5 weeks later, 10 September 1896

Catherine and I arrive back in London on a damp September morning. The sound of rain pattering against the window of our coach greets us as an old friend after the constant heat of Egypt.

The coach driver takes us from Victoria Station to Catherine's townhouse in Mayfair, located in the City of Westminster, close to Sir Stafford Northwind's office. I've only visited her Victorian house a couple of times, and she usually lives there on her own as Stafford prefers to stay in an apartment over his club.

Mayfair's grand squares, including its posh private garden squares, glimmer in the rain. The plants, the trees and the shrubbery look so fresh and alive after the dry, khaki-greens of the olive trees and sand-dust palms of Egypt.

The gentle tapping of droplets on the glass for once brings a sense of cosiness, a reassurance England is still

England and we're home, safe and sound. With a contented sigh, I pushed back further the lace curtain and peer out at St. George's, its sandy-white pillars momentarily transporting me back to Cairo. Then the Anglican church disappears as we turn into Grosvenor Street.

"Home," Catherine announces with joy in her voice as the horses draw to a stop outside her elegant three-storey, red-bricked house. Like Catherine, the house exudes an air of grandeur, of self-evident presence, a sure place in the world.

"I hope Franklin has lit the fires in my rooms," she says as we descend from the carriage holding our umbrellas over our heads, "or we're sure to freeze to death after the oven Egypt was. I've ordered him to prepare your rooms next to mine so we won't get lost in this place." Catherine looks up at her marital home and I see her think "for how long still?"

"I'm happy everywhere, Cathy, but I will only stay for a few days." I say as Jasper and I follow her up the steps to the sturdy wooden door, adorned with brass fittings and a recently polished knocker.

"I understand you want to go back to Honeydew Mansion, but now you're in London you simply must meet C." She looks back over her shoulder to me with a smile that says *we haven't trodden half the earth in search of this man to then let him escape one more time.*

"Is he still in London?"

Catherine shrugs, "he should be. I ordered him to stay put in my last letter but I'm not sure he's got it before we ourselves arrived."

The door is opened by a middle-aged gentleman who

must be the Franklin Catherine mentioned. He looks like a figure stepping right out of one of Charles Dickens's novels. The epitome of poise and propriety, Franklin has a commanding presence and a distinct air of formality.

My thoughts wander to my own Mrs Peaton at home with her flowery dresses, easy air, and the voice of a nightingale. The difference of circles Catherine and I frequent couldn't be more obvious. The man before us in his impeccable tailcoat, the silver-threaded hair slicked back neatly, and a pair of wire-rimmed spectacles on his nose, breathes the standard of a London butler in 1896.

"Lady Northwind, you have arrived safely. Everything is ready for you and Mrs Lynch. However, you have a visitor. I've let him into the parlour. Though I didn't have your permission to take a caller this early, I assumed you'd like to welcome Dr Cornelius Herriot on your return."

The butler's face is a testament to years of service and wisdom, knowing what his hosts need and when discretion is called for.

"Thank you, Franklin, most considerate of you. Can you see to it that our luggage is brought safely into the house?"

"Of course, Milady, and I'll have Regina serve your morning coffee as soon as you've settled in. I take it you had a pleasant return journey from Egypt, Milady?"

"Certainly Franklin, but it was tiresome to say the least, so please no callers for the rest of the day."

"Understood, Milady."

"I'll just freshen up and give you a moment together, alright?" I say before entering the lush boudoir Catherine has reserved for me.

"Would you, dear? That's ever so thoughtful of you. Come down in an hour, will you? I can't wait for you to get to know C."

After all we went through for the sake of Dr Cornelius Herriot, I'm more than mildly curious to meet the gentleman who's been the constant presence – both dark and light – over Catherine's and my trip to the land of the pharaohs. Who is this distinguished British Egyptologist, known to be a beacon of knowledge and academic brilliance amidst his contemporaries? But above all, who is this mysterious C who's captured my cousin's heart years ago and means the world to her?

For a moment I think I'm seeing a trick, with Ralph Herriot at the table. Then quick as it happens, I remember all this nonsense came about because they're identical twins, so clearly Cornelius looks like Ralph! In the chair, clad in a tailored suit, the dark hair combed, sand and bruises gone, sits Cornelius Herriot. As he rises from his chair, tall and lean as his brother, I spot the slight differences, mostly in demeanour and studiousness. Now I realize I overlooked the clues at the Shepheard's breakfast table where he sat reading The Times.

This is a different man, maybe the same deep-set hazel eyes and dark hair, but much more serious, with an aura of wisdom and study around him. How could I have missed it? I should have known he wasn't the Ralph Herriot I had seen parading through Dartmond's Darren Street with Winnifred hanging onto his arm.

"I'm sorry." I say as I shake his hand. Strong and warm.

"Sorry for what, Mrs Lynch?" The hazel eyes take me in with surprise. I study him intently. His face bears the evidence of many hours spent under the Egyptian sun. Lines at his eyes etched by the sands of time. His whole countenance, though dressed impeccably, including patterned waistcoat, a gold pocket watch, and even a silk scarf embroidered with hieroglyphs, breathes study and travel. This man is not the Cotswold's lavender factory owner with his quick quip and easy-go-lucky manners.

Then I shrug. "Well, I guess I couldn't have prevented the hostage-taking of your brother, should I have known it was you."

"Oh, my dear Mrs Lynch. You are indeed the detective Ralph told me you are. You're still breaking your head over the should and shouldn'ts of our recent rigmarole. Please don't. No one is to blame for what happened but these rapscallions. And we're all safe and can continue our work and not a dime was spent. I call that a marvellous feat."

"I guess you're right, Dr Herriot."

"Oh, do call me Cornelius, Mrs Lynch. I feel I owe you that after all you've done for my family and for dear Catherine."

"Then, please call me Imogene."

"Imogene it is!"

"Come and sit by the fire, Immy," Catherine pats the velvet fabric of the sofa next to her and I slip beside her. Cornelius takes up a seat opposite us, crossing his long legs and looking at us with a quizzical and warm glow in the light-brown eyes.

"Now, Imogene, tell me honestly. Would you terribly object to having a desert digger and sand explorer in your family?"

"Are you...?" I don't finish my sentence, staring in wonder from Catherine to Cornelius.

Catherine leans over and kisses my cheek.

"Yes," she squeals, "C has been so kind as to make Stafford's acquaintance after Winnifred agreed to a divorce. I know it's not how we are brought up, dear Cousin, but better be happy than in a miserable marriage, don't you agree? So, it's C & C from now on and for eternity."

"I'm quite beyond having judgments on people's marital status," I say. "I'm just relieved and so grateful we all made it out of Egypt alive. And that you, dear Cathy, can finally, finally be happy. That makes all we went through worth the agony. Congratulations to you both!"

Jasper runs around the room wildly wagging his tale and yapping as if he's seeing a hare up close.

"Champagne!" Catherine cries, ringing the service bell with all her might.

32

HOME IN LANDDULTON

Honeydew Mansion, 5 days later 15 September 1896

As Tomas, taciturn and wiry as ever, steers the Hansom with old Bella trotting ahead from Cheltenham Station to Honeydew Mansion, I inhale the mid-September Cotswolds' air with all my senses.

Home. We're almost home, Jasper!

Then why do I feel this strange kind of emptiness? After all the colours and spicy scents of Egypt, Landdulton looks...*dull*. I don't dare to say the word aloud, but it's how it feels. There's nothing wrong with the lovely English countryside experiencing an oh-so-gentle transition from summer to autumn.

What I see from my carriage window is what I need to see and love, picturesque landscapes, rolling hills, cute dainty houses. The colour mosaic of the leaves on the trees already begins to change, painting nature with shades of gold, red, and brown.

The air is crisp, the sun, sweet and mellow, rises higher, making the dewdrops glisten on the grass and spiderwebs as if dressing the meadows for a ball. Farmers and labourers are walking to their fields, carrying reeks and shovels and cows stand as if waiting for their portrait to be taken, still and dreamy. In the distance the sound of cowbells echoes across the green valleys, a very different call to prayer.

We pass villages, where I hear the familiar sounds of horse-drawn carriages pass by on cobblestone roads, not sand tracks, making the clip-clop of the horses' hooves a rhythmical, soothing stamp. Bella does her best to keep up with the tune.

I smell freshly baked bread waft from the open door of a bakery and watch shoppers hasting along the pavement to get to the market stalls before noon. It's all familiar and good but the hollowness in my heart returns.

Oh Thaddeus, this is your land, your home. But you're no longer here, I think not without melancholy. Jasper, always alert to my feelings, presses his warm snout to my legs.

"Yes, my darling Roly-Poly, we're almost there," I promise him and scan the coast of Tiversack Lake for the first glimpse of my red-roofed house.

There she is, clean and pristine and just as I left her. For the first time since the trip from Cheltenham my heart jumps up. It's good to be home. It will be a delight to take a rest. And to have Mrs Peaton and Bernie look after me. It's only then I remember my loyal housekeeper had told me she and the gardener had wedding plans. My Egyptian adventure had totally pushed that to the background.

"Well, more wedding bells to listen to," I tell myself chirpily.

"MRS LYNCH, OH-OH-OH!" Mrs Peaton stands in the doorway, drying her hands on her apron and looking dismayed. "I have been so worried about you! But here you are, looking slightly tanned and thank goodness, not underfed. What a nefarious trip that must have been."

I can't help but laugh, "good Heavens, Mrs Peaton, have you been reading the papers by any chance?"

"Not just that!" The housekeeper shakes her round face, the clear grey eyes taking me in inquiringly. "Mayor Banerjee has been to the house twice as well, asking after your well-being. That's when I really started to worry, you see." She bends to caress Jasper's white and tan head. "Oh, dearie and you being drawn into all that, you poor, poor thing."

"We're all alive and well, nobody kidnapped," I joke but the serious concern in my housekeeper brings home the danger we were in.

Well, what's life without a little spice? My Thaddeus seems to whisper in my ear as I follow Mrs Peaton into my spic and span dear home.

"Oh," I sigh with relief, "I'm never going to travel again in my life." But then there's that niggling thought

Catherine and I in fact had a great adventure and many wondrous moments in Egypt. There were days I hardly had the time to think of my benedict, whereas here in my wonderful home everything reminds me of him and of his absence. Oh, the duality of human existence. Well, I've got nothing to plan or worry about at the moment but enjoy my home and reminiscence on my whirlwind life of the past two months.

I'm so glad to be back in my own sitting room with its refined charm and timeless cosiness. Jasper races around the room and then puts his snout to the window overlooking the garden and the meadows beyond. I open the door for him, and he's gone. Chasing rabbits and sniffing hedgehogs. I see the white of his tail as he rushes through the tall grasses at the end of the garden.

Then I sit in my chair by the window with my eyes growing moist. It's all so familiar and so dear.

"Tea, Mrs Lynch? Proper English tea as it should be served?" Mrs Peaton asks.

"That would be delicious," I agree, "and the mail if you will, please."

As I sit waiting for my tea, I look around my sitting-room with joy. The walls with rich floral-patterned wallpaper add just the right touch of warmth and femininity to the room.

"Are you sure you want this wallpaper, my dear?" Thaddeus had implored, "you're not afraid you will tire of these daisies and cornflowers?"

"Will you?" I had replied.

"Heavens, darling, I wouldn't know a flowered wall from a striped one. You choose - I'm happy when you're happy."

"I've never known whether you hated the flower wallpaper, Thaddeus." I say aloud, "but at least you loved our large windows with heavy curtains. I've seen your face when you closed them at dusk."

And my benedict loved our fireplace, the focal point of the room, framed with carved oak and the backside with decorative tiles he chose himself. I can still see him poke that fire until the blazing wood crackled. Yes, my husband took pride in a good fire.

Next my eyes go to the mantelpiece with family portraits of both the Lynchs and the Bowditchs. My eyes stop at a photograph of Catherine and me in our teens, arms around each other's waists and smiling at my father who took the photograph.

"Cathy," I say, "oh Cathy, I'm so grateful you came back into my life. How I missed you all those years."

Mrs Peaton comes in with the tea and freshly baked buns. "Are you warm enough after that desert heat?" she asks, "or should I get you a stole?"

"I'm fine, Mrs Peaton. And how are you? How have you been?"

"Fine, fine! Bernie's been doing up the cottage for us and we've generally just kept busy doing what we're supposed to do, which is looking after Honeydew Mansion. But it's been a bit silent in the house, I must say.'

"When's the wedding?" I ask, accepting a cup of tea from her.

"Oh, we thought end of October, if that's alright with you?"

"Perfect!" I exclaim, "make sure you involve me in your plans. I want to make myself useful."

"I will, Mrs Lynch, don't worry. There's plenty still to

be done. Though it's only going to be a modest affair. And here's your mail. I've sorted it to date. I'll leave you to it for a moment but just ring the bell should you need me."

"Can you invite Bernie to dinner tonight? I think it would be lovely to have dinner together, just the three of us."

The grey eyes start to sparkle. "I'll ask him. I think he'd love that. It'll be roast chicken and potatoes. Nothing fancy but I made the cream custard pies you love for dessert."

"Sounds delicious!"

She looks at me as if I'm lying.

"I found my appetite in Cairo," I explain. Now my housekeeper looks bemused. "Oh, that's ... uh...exceptional."

Mrs Peaton is not an Egypt fan. One can tell that from a mile off.

I TURN to my tea and my mail. The first letter I open is one from Mayor Banerjee.

Dear Mrs. Lynch,

As I pen these lines, my heart finds solace in knowing that you are safely and comfortably within the confines of your Landdulton residence. This knowledge bestows a much-needed tranquility on my troubled mind.

I continue to find myself at a loss for adequate words to convey my remorse for the egregious error I committed by mistaking Dr Cornelius Herriot for his brother Ralph, and in so doing, imperiling you and your esteemed entourage during your sojourn in Egypt. I pray time shall witness the forgiveness of my misguided judgment.

Verily, I was woefully unaware of the existence of Mr Ralph Herriot's kin, a regrettable oversight on my part, considering the Herriot lineage spans several generations in Dartmond.

Furthermore, I confess my complete ignorance concerning the matrimonial union betwixt Mrs Winnifred Herriot and the aforementioned Dr Cornelius, for such an uncommon liaison is scarcely anticipated within the standards of our modest rural community.

Yet, in hindsight, I find myself condemning my own lack of prudence. A man of my station should have exercised utmost caution and propriety in matters of such significance. For this lack of discernment, I

again ask you my sincerest apologies,
entreating you, dear madam, to bestow upon
me the honor of a visit at your convenience,
that I may have the opportunity to express
my regrets in person.

> With the most profound affection,
> Mayor Rahul Banerjee.

> P.S. In addition to my sincerest apologies,
I beseech you to grant me the privilege of
discussing a matter of delicate import
concerning a cherished family heirloom. It is
held, against my late father's explicit wishes,
within the hallowed precincts of a Hindu
temple in Punjab. I implore you not to feel
rushed in this matter, for I trust in your
discernment to determine the most opportune
moment for such a discourse.

"OH NO," I cry out, "dear God in Heaven, not India! Not India!"

~

I HOPE YOU ENJOYED Imogene's adventurous trek to Egypt. Next she will be going to India, but for now she's taking a short break to enjoy her Honeydew Mansion in Landdulton and let Roly-poly Jasper chase rabbits around Tiversack Lake..

To find out when Imogene is going to India, please sign up for my newsletter here. You will get *The Disappearance of Miss Phoebe Hewlett* for free.

ABOUT THE AUTHOR

Historical mystery author Hannah Ivory's crib stood near the Seine in Paris, but she was raised in the south of Holland by Anglo-Dutch parents.

She writes quirky historical mysteries set in the late Victorian era under the pen name Hannah Ivory. *The Mrs Imogene Lynch Series* stars the kind but opinionated Victorian widow of Constable Thaddeus Lynch.

Under the nom de plume Hannah Byron, she writes her main body of work: inspirational historical fiction about the World Wars. The Hannah Ivory books are the light and fun detective books.

As an independent author, Hannah publishes both pen names with her own publishing firm *Hannah Byron Books*. The biggest advantage of self-publishing is always being close to the readers.

Strong women are at the core of Ivory's books in both genres. Every book is a tribute to the generations that started the liberation of women on the world stage.

Whether it's the traditionally thinking but curious widow Mrs Lynch, or the "resistance girls" in the world wars, who got dirty in overalls, flew planes, and did intelligence work. Today's girl bosses can but stand on the shoulders of their (great)grandmothers.

Side-by-side with their male counterparts, Ivory's heroines stand for freedom, equality and... love.

ALSO BY HANNAH IVORY
HISTORICAL MYSTERIES

The Mrs Imogene Lynch Series

The Unsolved Case of the Secret Christmas Baby

The Peculiar Vanishing Act of Mr Ralph Herriot

The Resistance Girl Series (Hannah Byron)

HISTORICAL FICTION

In Picardy's Fields

The Diamond Courier

The Parisian Spy

The Norwegian Assassin

The Highland Raven

The Crystal Butterfly

The London Spymaker (preorder)

The Agnès Duet (Hannah Byron)

Miss Agnes

Doctor Agnes